MB

PM

Ꮯ

Ꮯ

– ɓ

–

Tᵢ

THE INHERITANCE

Sara expects that when a local group of people from her village who want a say in the future of an empty manor house confront the new owners, her own loyalty will be clear and simple — but that's before she is unexpectedly chosen to talk things over with the new owner, Madame Jannet Rogard, and her attractive son, Nick, at their château in France. What's more, even though Sara and Nick come from different worlds, there's no denying the attraction growing between them . . .

Books by Wendy Kremer
in the Linford Romance Library:

REAP THE WHIRLWIND
AT THE END OF THE RAINBOW
WHERE BLUEBELLS GROW WILD
WHEN WORDS GET IN THE WAY
COTTAGE IN THE COUNTRY
WAITING FOR A STAR TO FALL
SWINGS AND ROUNDABOUTS
KNAVE OF DIAMONDS
SPADES AND HEARTS
TAKING STEPS
I'LL BE WAITING
HEARTS AND CRAFTS
THE HEART SHALL CHOOSE
THE HOUSE OF RODRIGUEZ
WILD FRANGIPANI
TRUE COLOURS
A SUMMER IN TUSCANY
LOST AND FOUND
TOO GOOD TO BE TRUE
UNEASY ALLIANCE
IN PERFECT HARMONY

WENDY KREMER

THE INHERITANCE

Complete and Unabridged

LINFORD
Leicester

First published in Great Britain in 2015

First Linford Edition
published 2017

A catalogue record for this book is available
from the British Library.

ISBN 978–1–4448–3402–4

Published by
F. A. Thorpe (Publishing)
Anstey, Leicestershire

Set by Words & Graphics Ltd.
Anstey, Leicestershire
Printed and bound in Great Britain by
T. J. International Ltd., Padstow, Cornwall

This book is printed on acid-free paper

1

Dominique Rogard read the letter and handed it back to his mother. He shrugged his shoulders and ran his hands through his hair. His eyes were dark grey, almost black. 'And what do you plan to do with it?'

Jannet smiled. 'I haven't decided yet. I suppose we'll do what most people do with an unexpected inheritance. To be honest, I'd almost forgotten about Maldon House. Since your gran died, no one has been there. That's at least seven or eight years ago. I don't think you ever went there, did you?'

He shook his head and stuck his hands into his work-marked jeans. 'Gran wanted to take me a couple of times, but something always got in the way. I could never go when she wanted to go, because of school. I was in hospital once, and I remember another

1

time when I spent the summer learning to sail with André. After I went to agricultural college, I never had a lot of spare time. You went quite often with Gran, didn't you? What's it like?'

Jannet looked past him out of the window. 'It's a beautiful house. One of those old English manor houses you see in the glossy magazines, surrounded by a big park-like garden. I was there once when the bluebells bloomed and it was unbelievable.'

'And your uncle didn't have any other relatives?'

'I think he had a cousin somewhere in Scotland, but he didn't like him and they quarrelled constantly.'

Dominique lifted his dark brows. 'So he left it to you. Pretty stupid thing to do, if you ask me! You live in France. What did he expect you to do, leave here and move there?'

'I expect he hoped that someone in the family would fall in love with it and take care of it. It seems we own it now.'

'You own it. It's nothing to do with me.'

'Oh, don't be silly, Nick. We're in this together. Selling does seem to be the logical thing to do, but I don't know how to go about that. Perhaps there's another alternative to selling it? After all, we aren't desperate for money in the way we were four years ago.'

'Like for instance?'

'Renting it out to someone. You could use it as a holiday home when you get married.'

He burst out laughing and showed even, white teeth in a tanned face. It was clear just by looking at his broad shoulders and slim hips that he was someone who spent most of his time outdoors.

'Mother! You never give up, do you? We work day and night just to keep this place going. How are we going to manage a house in England — fly back and forth every weekend? And stop hassling me about a wife! Women like clothes and a good time, and insist on instant home improvements.' He glanced around the room. 'Heaven knows the château needs some renovation, but only when time and money allow.'

She sighed. 'I know. Your father shouldn't have poured all the profits into the estate like he did. You know we always intended to modernize the house after he'd paid for the machinery and all the rest, but he didn't reckon with a heart attack. He increased the value of the estate, but pushed up the inheritance tax. We're doing fine. The rooms we decorated last winter look really good. And there are lots of local girls who are waiting for a wink from you. They ask about you every time I meet them. And what about Madeleine?'

He considered her twinkling eyes and ran his long fingers through his unruly black hair. 'Madeleine is a friend, nothing more. I keep telling you that. I've no plans to change my single status.'

Jannet looked down at the sheet of

paper. 'Well, perhaps this will help solve any present economic problems.'

He looked at his watch. 'Think it over and let me know what you'd like to do. I'll help in any way I can, of course. It's your inheritance, your decision. Will you have to go to England to sort it out?'

'I have no idea! I feel guilty because we didn't keep in regular contact with Uncle Colin. I didn't even know he was ill. I hope he wasn't lonely and neglected when he died. I'll get in touch with this lawyer to find out what I have to do.'

'Do that! We'll talk about it later on. I planned to meet André this evening, but he's promised to do something for his gran, so I'll be home instead. I'm off to the top field now to check the artichokes. I reckon it is only a matter of days before we can start to harvest. The sooner we send them to the markets, the better.'

'Bring me a couple for tomorrow's lunch, and don't be late for dinner! I'll find some photos of Maldon House to show you later on, so that you know what I'm talking about.'

'What are we having tonight?'

'Corn chicken!'

He gave her a warm smile. 'I'll be on time. I wouldn't miss your chicken and potato wedges for the world. I'm already hungry.'

She gave him an affectionate tap on his arm. 'Get along with you. And don't get so wrapped up in your work again that you forget the time and spoil my cooking. Six-thirty on the dot!'

With long strides, Dominique left her holding the letter and reminiscing about Maldon House. Jannet remembered her uncle; he was kind and benevolent. She'd even been friendly with a couple of the village children one summer when she stayed there.

A short time later, while checking the state of the well-cared-for field of plump artichokes, Dominique mused that his mother's unexpected inheritance would take the pressure off things.

It was hers — he didn't want it, but he knew that in an emergency she would loan him her last penny. His father had transferred ownership of the farm to him not long before he died. He'd hoped it would help reduce inheritance tax, but his death was too soon and it left Dominique with a sizeable sum to pay instead. He was almost forced to sell some of the estate to pay it off. He'd manage to scratch it together with his own meagre funds, the help of his bank manager, and his mother's savings. He'd made real inroads into the bank repayments, and also managed some home improvements in the winter when there was less work around the estate. It had been a big challenge ever since he took over, but he liked challenges. He found that he relished winning and solving difficulties.

Movement in one of the distant fields caught his attention. His eyes narrowed and he soon figured out who was hurrying in the direction of the house. He lifted his hand to Madeleine, and she waved back. Her parents' farm bordered their land. He'd known her all his life and liked her. He recalled his mother's hints about marriage, and how she'd mentioned Madeleine. Could you base a marriage on mere friendship? Madeleine would inherit her parents' farm one day, but he had land enough. And even if he wanted to, he wasn't in a financial position to marry. He didn't believe in romance, but marriage for the wrong reasons was wrong too. Many of his friends had rushed into marriage, and were already facing divorce. Better to stay single than fool yourself that you'd found the perfect woman, when in reality she was just second best. Perhaps he'd end up like his unknown great-uncle in England, and would bequeath his property to some distant relative who wouldn't know what to do with it. He scrambled down from the tractor, and with his pocketknife he cut through the thick stalks of a couple of fat artichokes for tomorrow.

2

Sara looked up, and her brown eyes twinkled as she studied Eddie Protheroe. Her shoulder length nut-brown hair swayed as she shook her head. 'You don't need to remind me. I look forward to it every week. You know that!'

'Yes I do, but you're the best in the group. Even my most talented pupils in the upper forms didn't have the feel for French that you do.'

Colour heightened her cheeks. 'That's because I love French and always have. It was one of my best subjects in school. It's such a romantic language. I liked other languages, and managed Italian quite well, but French was always my favourite.'

Eddie Protheroe ran a hand over his face. His blue eyes sparkled below bushy white eyebrows. 'You should have gone to university. It's a disgrace that your aunt put her foot down. You would've done well, and you'd have made a good teacher.'

'Aunt Hilda has cared for me since I was six, Eddie. University would only have been a continued drain on her income. Even if I went to a local university and lived at home, the tuition fees are a horror. She deserves a break.'

'Hmm! I wouldn't be surprised, with your grades, if you'd been able to get a scholarship or some kind of special grant. I don't think she even tried to find out.'

Sara smiled, and loose tendrils of shiny hair escaped and softened her expression. 'I'm not unhappy, Eddie. I like my job in the library, and I'm earning money for the first time in my life. After giving Aunt Hilda a little housekeeping money, I can do what I like with the rest.'

'Hilda's earning good money as a headmistress. She's managed without any extra from you until now. Why does she need board money? She never goes anywhere, she never does anything, she has no hobbies, and she wears clothes that went out with the dodo.'

'Perhaps it's because she enjoys economizing. Some people do. I don't mind, Eddie; in fact, it makes me feel better. Once I've passed my driving test — soon, I hope — I'm intending to save for furniture and get my own flat.' Sara wanted to get him off the subject of Aunt Hilda. Eddie was also a teacher, an ex-teacher, and he felt no empathy for her aunt. 'Are we in the reading room?'

'Yes, seven o'clock as usual.'

'What's the theme tonight?'

He waved his finger. 'No cheating! You'll find out at the same time as everyone else.'

Sara stacked his books and handed them over. 'It's interesting to talk in French about up-to-date news. The books we had in school were often out of date. I think I'd forget a lot of my

French if we didn't have our conversation group.'

He laughed softly. 'I enjoy it as much as you do, and it keeps me on my toes. It's rewarding to see how everyone's confidence is growing. Brian used to be afraid to open his mouth, but these days he joins in, and doesn't mind much anymore if his grammar isn't always correct.'

'Yes, he knows we're all grasping for the right words most of the time. No one makes fun of each other. We know you'd soon put a stop to that. It's good fun, even if you have to keep prompting us and supplying new vocabulary and a new subject every week. It keeps our brains ticking over. We read the French approach. Sometimes it's very different to what we read in English newspapers.'

Eddie hoisted the books under his arm. 'What about the Maldon House protest? Are you coming?'

'It's on Thursday, isn't it? Yes, of course. I love Maldon House. The garden and grounds are beautiful. I heard that someone's interested in part of the land for building a couple of houses.'

He nodded. 'It's shocking! If they wanted to build on the outskirts of the grounds and needed an extra couple of yards, nobody would make such a fuss. But they're trying to get building permission to build ten ultra-modern houses on the rise behind the house. It'll ruin the whole place, and there's no earthly reason to do that. I expect they're hoping to get the ground cheaply.'

Sara clenched her mouth tighter. 'Is it certain that it's going to be sold? Mr Harper never minded village kids on the grounds. He said it kept the weeds down. We loved playing there.'

'There's never smoke without fire. I only found out about the possibility that someone might build houses there by chance when I was talking to Bob White in the pub. He works for Watson's, and he said they had their eye on the place. They're already trying to find out what's happening, in case there's a chance of buying some ground. We'll remind the building authorities about the bluebell wood, and perhaps there are special insects or animals there. We need ammunition for the list of our objections.'

'Watson's? Never heard of them,' Sara said.

'It's a fairly new company with headquarters out on the Flaxton road. They build expensive, exclusive sorts of houses — all straight lines, steel and glass.'

Looking quite determined, Sara said., 'Well, we can try to put a spoke in their wheels, can't we?'

He nodded in agreement. 'It's all conjecture and assumption at the moment, but the sooner we show them we're involved, the better. See you later, Sara!' He lifted his free hand as he went towards the door.

Sara started to replenish the shelves with returned books. As she moved around the room, pushing the trolley

14

and fitting the books into their appropriate slots on the shelves, she thought about Eddie and his protest group. He lived near Aunt Hilda's cottage and had always had time for a chat and an encouraging word as she was growing up. He had his own family, but like the other villagers, he had a soft spot for the little girl with the heart-shaped face and sunny smile who had come to live with her aunt after her mother was killed in a road accident and left her an orphan. Eddie had encouraged her interest in languages and history, the subjects he taught at the local grammar school. She could picture his domed head crowned with thick white hair and his bright blue eyes. He'd never lost the knack of unbounded enthusiasm for whatever interested him, and he was always keen to do anything that was good for the community. His children had left home years ago and were scattered far afield. His wife had died unexpectedly a couple of years ago, and although he

and his children had a good relationship, he'd decided to stay in his cottage.
He managed very well on his own, with
the aid of a daily helper.

Sara also thought about the large
manor house on the fringe of the
village. She couldn't imagine how
Maldon House and its gardens would
look if houses were built on the rise at
the back. It was worth protesting about,
even if Aunt Hilda insisted that it was
all a waste of time and that money
always won in the end.

★   ★   ★

That evening's French conversation
was fun. They'd been meeting for
several months, and by now everyone
thought it was an enjoyable and
instructional hour. Some of them were
there to improve their school French
for spending holidays in France. Brian
was planning to buy a holiday home in
Provence and wanted to be able to
make himself understood when that

happened. Derek was a local wine dealer who had frequent contact with wine growers in the Bordeaux region; he wanted a better command of the language to feel at ease when he had to negotiate. Mrs Mortimer came along to show the others that she'd been educated in a Swiss boarding school. Her French was effortless, but she was full of her own importance, and the others tended to ignore her as much as they could without being pointedly rude. Sara, however, had no special reason to be there. She just liked French.

Walking home with Eddie afterwards, she looked up at the clear night sky with its sprinkling of stars. Their footsteps echoed in the dark. 'That was fun Eddie — the article about how Europe used to be before the European Market, and what it's like today, was spot on.'

'Yes, I thought it was fun to read when I spotted it in *Questions Internationales*. The vocabulary wasn't too difficult, and I thought the bit about how people were happy with just plain coffee years ago and now expect dozens of variations was really funny and very true. Although I don't think that's anything to do with the European Market.'

Sara chuckled. 'No, it's the result of affluence. You have to know exactly what you want these days if you buy coffee. The list is never-ending.'

They'd reached Aunt Hilda's, and the curtain in the lighted window twitched as they stood and said goodnight. Eddie nodded in the direction of the cottage. 'It'd do her some good to get out a bit more. She never goes anywhere, does she?'

Sara shrugged. 'She's happy enough, Eddie. She goes to church on Sunday, and the occasional concert, but she always tells me she has to prepare her lessons and do corrections whenever I suggest something.'

'Huh! She's been teaching for donkey's years. If she can't teach without hours of preparation by now, she never will. The contents of a subject and method of teaching do change with the passing of time, but not that much. She's not a trainee teacher anymore! I have no patience with the woman. Anyway, goodnight Sara! I'll see you on Thursday?'

'Yes. In the parish hall?'

He nodded in the semi-darkness. 'I'm going to try to find out who owns Maldon House before then. I remember that old Harper did have occasional visitors, but it didn't happen often. There were some French relatives, but I haven't heard anything about them for years. Recently, just the upkeep of the place drained him. I think he felt too ill to be bothered to contact anyone. He loved the place. He wasn't married and he had no children, so it must have gone to a distant relative. That's not so good. Someone who isn't attached to the house, or the village, is more likely to want to sell it fast and ignore the objections. Whoever owns it now might even encourage that building scheme.'

'If the builders still haven't got permission, that'll gives us a little leeway. If we don't do anything and don't protest, it'll just be a walkover. I can't imagine what ultra-modern houses perched behind the mansion would be like. Horrible, I imagine.' Sara sighed. 'It must be difficult to sell a place that size these days, especially one with so much land around it.'

'If the new owner gets enough money for building plots, they might not worry so much about the rest. If they sell the section behind the house, what's stopping them selling off the part near the stream, or chopping the wood down to build a supermarket?'

'Don't Eddie! It doesn't bear thinking about!'

'It's early days yet. Perhaps it's all hot air. We have to find out exactly what's going on first. We'll take one step at a time, and fight them all the way if necessary. Houses on that spot would ruin the whole look of the place, and ultimately the village would change completely too.'

3

The handful of people in the village hall listened to Eddie's explanations and slowly began to understand what they were taking on. Eddie said he was on the verge of finding out the name of the new owners. He was also in contact with the appropriate department of the local council, and he already had an appointment with the management of the building company that was showing interest in a plot of land. Despite a little reluctance on Tom Willow's part, Eddie persuaded the man to accompany him to meet with the various people. Eddie reassured Tom he wouldn't need to argue, but just be there, as more than one person always looked better when community matters and protests were in the making.

Sara sat next to Kelly, a friend from her schooldays. The fact that they both came from the village and were the same age meant that they'd travelled to school together. They'd been in parallel classes, and their daily meet-up had automatically fated them to friendship. On the bus Sara had generally been the listener, while Kelly had always been more boisterous and ready for a fresh adventure. Aunt Hilda didn't approve of Kelly because the girl tried to look sexy in her school uniform. Secretly Sara thought she'd been successful, but never said so to her aunt. Out of school, Kelly's clothes were also showy and garish. The two girls had rarely gone out together when they were growing up because of Aunt Hilda's disapproval.

Kelly's tastes had mellowed since those days, but she was still a dramatic picture. She had blond hair, bluebell-blue eyes, a curvy figure, and a peachy complexion. She liked tight skirts and figure-hugging tops, and she never lacked boyfriends. These days Kelly was chief secretary to the director of a local glass factory. She talked constantly about finding a 'better' job, but didn't do anything about looking for one. And she already had her own flat, a two-room apartment over the local post office. She'd left home when she started working, and since then she'd lived her own life in her own idiosyncratic style.

She tried continually to change Sara's style of dressing, but Sara didn't give in. She knew she'd never feel happy wearing the kinds of clothes Kelly suggested, and she also knew that lots of makeup wouldn't make her feel happier either. Sara knew that her own taste suited her character much better than Kelly's suggestions. She was a straightforward, pleasant person with a good, slim figure, who was fond of items that she could match and mix with new additions and that weren't out of fashion six weeks later. Because they understood each other so well, Kelly was never offended when Sara rejected her ideas.

Sara's boyfriends never lasted long

because she was a romantic who was hoping to find the love of a lifetime. Kelly's didn't either, because they bored her in a matter of days, and she was only interested in having fun with no strings attached.

Sara couldn't remember her father. He'd been an unknown Welsh artist who'd died of pneumonia after he'd been painting winter landscapes of Snowdonia in the driving wind and rain. Her mother had tried to dissuade him, but he wanted the paintings to bring him some longed-for recognition at last. Sara's memories of her mother had faded a little too. There weren't many photos, and Sara treasured the ones she had. Aunt Hilda seldom mentioned either of them. Sara did remember how her mother had spoken with love in her eyes about her father as Sara sat on her knee, or when she was putting Sara to bed. Sara wanted a love like that, one that survived the greatest disasters that could happen to any loving couple. Sometimes she wondered what her life would have been like if they hadn't died and she hadn't been left to Aunt Hilda's care. Thankfully her innate positive attitude to life had helped her cope with the disappointment of not having parents like all the rest of her friends as she grew up. She'd learned it was up to her to make the best she could out of any situation.

She nudged Kelly's whispering into silence after Eddie looked in their direction a couple of times with his jaw clenched and his eyes slightly narrowed. They listened as various people gave their personal views. An hour later Eddie declared the meeting closed, and reminded everyone to come to the meeting on Sunday afternoon so that he could pass on the results from his investigations. There were a couple of groans, but nearly everyone agreed to come — as long as it didn't last too long.

★　★　★

On Sunday Eddie informed them that the council hadn't yet given building permission, and so far no one had applied for it. He now knew who owned Maldon House — a niece of Mr Harker's who lived in France — and he'd persuaded the building company to send a representative to talk to them about their plans. Eddie added that they guessed the villagers were worried, and he thought they wanted to counter any opposition early on.

One villager raised his finger. 'Wouldn't it be a good idea for someone to talk to the new owner?'

Eddie nodded. 'I thought of that too, Jack, but personally I think telephone conversations are never very satisfactory. You seldom get the information you want, and you don't get an impression of how things really are going unless you are face to face.'

'Then why don't you go to France and talk to them? The language is no problem for you, and you have plenty of spare time. Most of us are tied down with our jobs.'

Eddie looked uncertain. 'I could, of course, but I wouldn't like to do it on my own. I'd need someone else with me to make the visit a formal one. I could manage a weekend, I suppose, if someone volunteers to come with me.'

Sara's mind whizzed around. What a great chance to go to France! She was just about to offer when Kelly jumped up and beat her to the post.

'I'll come with you, Eddie! I can take my holidays when I like. We could even go midweek if you want. I haven't got any other plans this year so far. It'll give me a chance to stock up on French perfume and cosmetics, if they're cheaper. My French isn't up to much, but that's no problem. You'll be doing all the talking.'

The audience chuckled. Eddie looked perplexed, and Sara could tell he was fighting an inclination to refuse outright, but he was too polite and didn't want to give the impression that he was choosy about who supported the group or not. He cleared his throat. 'That's very good of you, Kelly. When I've thought out some definite plans, I'll let you know.'

Someone said, 'Aye aye, anything brewing between you two? After his money, are you, Kelly?'

There was another bout of laughter. Eddie rustled his papers, looking ill at ease, and said, 'The building company's offered to send a junior manager along to our meeting one evening next week. I suggested Wednesday. I hope that's agreeable for everyone?' There were a couple of mumbles, but in the end no one objected. 'Right! That's it for this afternoon. Thanks for coming, everyone. Things are moving and we're on our way.'

They gathered their belongings, and still chatting, began to file out. As Kelly headed for the exit, she asked Sara, 'Coming? I'm going into town. I'm meeting some friends in the bistro, and we'll go to the cinema or on to the pub after.'

Sara shook her head. 'No, thanks. It's good of you to offer, but you know what happened last time. You wanted to stay longer, and I was dead beat and wanted to go home. As you were the only one with a car, I spoiled your evening.'

Kelly rummaged in her bag as she stood in the porch-way, then refreshed her lipstick. 'It was no problem! I always stay out too long, and too often. Sometimes I turn up for work feeling like death warmed up. But you don't go out often enough! Life passes by so fast. You'll end up like your Aunt Hilda if you're not careful. Are you sure you won't come?'

Sara smiled at her. 'Sure! Thanks anyway.'

'Toodle-oo! I'll see you Wednesday at the next showing with this lot. Sometimes I wondered why I bothered to join. I don't intend to spend the rest of my life in this place, and I'm not very interested in Maldon House, but then something like the chance of an unexpected trip to France comes up and I see why it was worthwhile coming.'

Sara tried to feel pleased for her. It was difficult because she was envious. 'Yes, I'll see you Wednesday. Don't forget to bring your library books with you. They're three weeks overdue, remember?'

'Will do!' Kelly was halfway down the flagged pathway. 'I never have time to finish them before the time runs out.' She waved her hand above her head.

Sara watched Kelly's departing figure until she reached her bright yellow Mini. She was so flamboyant. She knew how to enjoy life with no holds barred, and she accepted any negative consequences and criticism with aplomb.

Eddie was behind her, locking the door. Sara nodded in Kelly's direction. 'She's a handful, but I like her.'

He laughed. 'Yes, she certainly is a firework. A day or two in France with that young lady will be full of surprises. Ready?'

She nodded, and they set off together. 'Do you know anything about this niece who's inherited the manor?' Sara asked. 'Where does she live in France?'

'I didn't want to go into too many details just now, but to be honest, there's a very good chance that I know her.'

'Really?'

He nodded. 'I think she visited the place a couple of times with her mother. Some of the village children, including me, met her in the garden. She was glad of younger company, and we sometimes went over to play croquet or tennis.'

'Gosh! How old were you?'

He ran his hand over his chin. 'We were teenagers. I must have been fourteen or fifteen. She was a year or two younger. She was a pretty girl who spoke quite good English. Her mother was Mr Harper's sister. You can imagine that we boys thought she was quite exotic and were very impressed.

We'd never met a French girl before.'

'But isn't it extraordinary that now you're organizing the protest about Maldon House's future, she turns out to be the person who'll have the final word, and you already know her?'

'Yes, isn't it? I didn't want to broadcast it to everyone this afternoon. People will automatically think I'll have an easy time of it and come to a quick agreement of some kind. They might even stop coming to the protest meetings, and that would be bad. I haven't seen her since those days, and she might have changed a lot. She might not even remember me.'

'Well, you'll soon find out if you do visit her.'

He nodded. 'I'm also interested in what this chap from the building company has to say for himself next week. I don't intend to make another move until we've heard from him. They can't apply for building permission if they haven't bought the property, so nothing will happen overnight. It depends what the company plans and how they intend to go about it. Somehow I don't think they've contacted the new owner yet either. Anyway, they didn't mention it to us when we were there.'

'What's her name, this owner in France?'

'Rogard. Jannet Rogard. She lives in Brittany. I asked the lawyers for her address. They were reluctant to give it to me, but when I explained I was an old friend and would like to get in touch with her again for sentimental reasons, they softened up and gave in.'

'You could charm the hind leg off a horse!'

He laughed. 'You have to keep at it, Sara! If you give up at the first hurdle, you'll never complete the course. There's always a second route to get to your final destination. I looked up where she lives on the map. Funnily enough, someone I met when I was at university lives quite close by. If I go over, I'll get in touch with him, and hopefully I can pop in for a chat.' His eyebrows lifted. 'I'll do that when Kelly goes in search of cosmetics. If she thinks I'm going to waste my time in a shop being a translator, she can think again.'

Sara chuckled. 'Her French was never any good in school. In fact, it was abominable. I'd like to be a fly on the wall when she tries to explain what she wants.' She tilted her head to the side. 'But on the other hand, knowing Kelly, she'll manage somehow. She'll get by with hands and feet, blinking her eyelashes, and assuming her accustomed role of blameless naivety. It works every time!'

4

On Wednesday evening most of the protesters assembled in the community hall again. There was a buzz of conversation, and people stirred uneasily on their chairs waiting for the representative of Watson's Building Co. to arrive. Sara was near the back of the group. She kept a place free for Kelly, who finally dashed in with her silk scarf flying out behind her and clutching an enormous red leather bag.

Their guest speaker was the last to arrive. Mark Watson gave the gathering a brief glance before he spotted Eddie on the podium and hurried towards him, a smart leather briefcase in his hand.

Kelly nudged Sara. 'I say! Look at him! If that's one of the managers, the world of building is certainly improving.'

Sara wanted to chuckle but she didn't. Mark Watson was very good-looking, and was impeccably dressed in a designer suit and matching shirt and tie. He had blond hair and piercing blue eyes. He eyed the seated audience, and Sara wondered if it was only her imagination, or whether his glance really did linger a little longer on the two of them than on the other people.

Eddie used a gavel to silence the chatterers. 'Ladies and gentlemen, I'd like to introduce Mark Watson. He's a junior partner in Watson's Building Company, and has kindly agreed to come and enlighten us about their intentions regarding house-building on the grounds of Maldon House.'

There was a light round of applause, and Mark nodded appreciatively. 'Thank you, Mr Protheroe. I must admit that my company was surprised the other day when you paid us a visit to ask about our building plans for Maldon House. We were quite startled to find that something that we'd only discussed vaguely was being talked about in public, and that it was causing a hue and cry. You all realize that, just like any other company, we're in business to make money. Without going into too much detail, our company specializes in exclusive construction work. Our designs are individual and select. We try, wherever possible, to construct them in suitable settings. We're continually on the lookout for appropriate sites, and when we heard that the owner of Maldon House had died, we naturally wondered if it might be a spot for one of our schemes. I must emphasize it's a consideration and hasn't gone beyond the discussion stage. I gather from Mr Protheroe that some of you are already worried in case any changes we make detract from the village. Well you have my word that that won't happen. Even if we did want to build at Maldon House, the process is always a long and complex one. You'd have plenty of time to iron out any problems with us in advance.'

Kelly nudged Sara. 'Hasn't he got a lovely voice? What a man! He must be bright if he's already a junior partner. I bet that he's only a couple of years older than we are. I wonder if he's married.'

Whispering, Sara answered, 'Kelly, please remember we're here because of Maldon House, and not for you to pursue Mark Watson.'

'All's fair in love and war! I'm glad I came.'

Sara sighed and listened as Eddie asked Mark fielded questions. One man in the audience asked, 'We've heard that the houses you build are very modern in style. Don't you think that'd clash with Maldon House's appearance?'

'Time waits for no man, circumstances change, and necessity changes too,' Mark answered. 'Not many people can afford to buy places like Maldon House and its grounds as it stands these days. If it can't be sold in one piece, it might have to be chopped up into plots.'

'What about the look of the place? Will you take the wishes of the local community into account if you build there?'

Mark shrugged. 'Nothing's been settled. We'll cross that bridge when we come to it. A lot can be achieved by planting trees and restructuring the terrain. We've handled all kinds of similar construction work in the past, and everyone was satisfied with the results.'

'I'm sure you'll understand when I say that's hard for us to believe right now,' the man in the audience persisted. 'If the rise behind the house is covered in houses, planting trees won't hide them. I'm also sure any buyers will want a clear view and not tree trunks in front of their windows.'

Mark looked directly at the audience. 'I assure you that if . . . and it is still a big if . . . we do consider buying and building on ground in Maldon House, we'll do our best to take the wishes of local inhabitants into account.'

There were a few unbelieving jeers. Mark ignored them. 'If it helps, I'm quite prepared to show you what we've achieved in similar situations. You're welcome to view some of our past projects with me. You only need to get in touch, and we'll settle a time and a place.'

After some further questions about the company and what they were building at the moment, Eddie thanked him, and then said that unless someone had a pertinent question about something else to do with the present discussion, the meeting was closed for the evening. He reminded everyone that it would be sensible to elect a working committee so that decisions made in the general meetings could be followed up as soon as possible. People stood in groups talking for a while, and Eddie stopped here and there to chat.

Sara waited for Eddie to remind him that he hadn't told anyone when the next meeting would take place. Kelly had her eye on Mark at the podium. He was stuffing some notes into his briefcase. The two men came down the central aisle together and shook hands near the doorway.

Sara stopped Eddie. 'When's the next meeting?'

He hurried to shout to the remaining people. 'Next meeting, same time next week! If you know anyone who's already left, please tell them! Thanks for coming, everyone.' He turned to Sara again. 'Thanks, I nearly forgot. We'll have to get a committee organized soon. We can't call general meetings every couple of days. People will get fed up and drop out. Most of the things can be sorted out by a couple of enthusiastic workers, but they need general approval and authority. Then we only need to call everyone together to tell them what's happening and hear any new suggestions and ideas.'

Sara nodded and walked alongside him towards the door. Kelly was already there, flashing her eyes in Mark's direction. He looked back at Eddie briefly and raised his hand. Sara joined Kelly, who now was waiting for her with heightened colour and twinkling eyes. They started off down the pathway.

Kelly couldn't wait to enthuse about Mark. 'He's really nice. He asked me where I work and if I live in the village.'

Sara saw the warning signals. 'Kelly, he was only representing his company. He wasn't looking for a girlfriend. He may be married.'

'He isn't. I mentioned that I usually go into town for fun because there's nothing much for young people to do around here. He said he could understand that, as he always had to go elsewhere to make friends away from the company because of his family. I then asked him quite casually if he was married, and he said no! I said I'd be very interested in seeing one of the projects they've completed.' She waved a visiting card. 'He gave me his card and said I could call him anytime!'

Sara laughed. 'You are incorrigible!'

Mark drove past them in his Porsche and Kelly waved enthusiastically. He waved back from within the depths of the car.

★ ★ ★

The following week they elected a committee. There weren't as many people as there had been at the first meeting, and Sara remembered Eddie's comments about how too many meetings, too often, would drive people away. Eddie was elected chairman, while Tom Willows, Stan Ward the local butcher, and Sara were voted in as committee members. Eddie promised to make a membership list so that everyone would be kept informed of any progress, or invited to come to a general meeting for approval and sanction if they needed it.

Sara wasn't particularly anxious to be on the committee, but it was hard to find anyone who was prepared to help, so she gave in.

Eddie stated that he was thinking of making the trip to France the following week. Kelly wasn't present, but he would sort it out with her as soon as possible. After the meeting, he asked Sara to contact her and tell her to get in touch with him.

Next evening, Sara went round to Kelly's flat after work. Pop music was already audible when she went up the stairs to the door. Kelly flung it open and smiled at her. 'Come in! I was just making a meal. Want some?'

Sara glanced at a dinner plate with slices of fresh apples and chunks of cheese on a side table next to the couch. She shook her head. 'That's not a meal, that's a snack. No thanks, I've eaten already — a proper meal.'

'Don't gripe! I usually have a meal in the canteen at work. Now and then I skip it. You have to think of your figure!' She patted her flat stomach. 'So, to what do I owe the honour of your company? You don't come here often. Not often enough, I may add.'

'Eddie wants you to call him to sort out the details of the trip. He was talking about Friday to Sunday,' Sara explained.

'I can't!' Kelly popped another piece of apple in her mouth and crunched it.

'What?'

'I can't go.'

'Why not?'

'I've arranged to go to see one of Mark's projects next Friday, and he suggested we could make a proper trip out of it. Stay overnight.' Noticing her raised eyebrows, Kelly added, 'It's not like you think. All above board — separate rooms, separate bills, etcetera. Although I won't fight him for the restaurant bill.'

'And what about Eddie and the trip to France to meet Maldon House's new owner?'

Kelly shrugged. 'If he's set on going next weekend, he'll have to find someone else. Why don't you go? You're better suited anyway. You speak proper French, and you get on with Eddie. You also care more about the whole Maldon House affair than I do.'

Agog at the idea, Sara uttered, 'Me?'

'You'd be a damned sight more useful to him than Tom Willows would be. Tom's a treasure in his way, but he's very slow on the uptake, isn't he?'

Sara was overjoyed, but she didn't want to show too much enthusiasm. That might encourage Kelly to think twice about refusing. 'You're sure about not being able to go?'

'I just told you so. I'd rather spend the weekend with Mark Watson than with Eddie Protheroe. Anyone with sense would.' Realizing that sounded a bit offensive, she backpedalled. 'I don't mean you're stupid, love; I just mean it looking at it from my point of view. You didn't fancy Mark from the word go — I did.'

'I hope you do intend to look at this building scheme properly and tell us all about it afterwards,' Sara said. 'About the surroundings, about the way it's been integrated into the site, if there's anything similar to Maldon House nearby, that sort of thing.'

Looking at her red-tipped fingertips, Kelly said, 'I will. I can't promise my report will be full of vital information, because I don't recognize a steeple from a pigsty. But I'll get Mark to give me some descriptions, and I'll look out for things that stick out like a sore thumb. I could take some photos, OK?'

Sara nodded reluctantly.

'Good, that's settled then. You'll be going to France with Eddie, and I'm going to some place near Warminster with Mark.' She patted the cushion on the seat of a nearby chair. 'Come and make yourself comfortable. They're showing *Pretty Woman* with Richard Gere again. I love it. Here have a piece of cheese. It's Chester and cost me a bomb.'

5

Sara leaned on the ship's railing and looked at the choppy grey waves down below. It was exhilarating to think that she was on her way to France with Eddie. Her replacement was in charge of the library for the day. Aunt Hilda had fussed about the previous night, giving her unwanted advice about what and what not to do. Sara had let her carry on. It was always the same with Aunt Hilda — as soon as Sara was about to go off on her own, all kinds of catastrophes were imagined and solutions suggested. When she did finally get away; it was a relief, and she had a feeling of freedom. She never worried about something going wrong; she was on her way to France, not a war zone.

The heavy iron door behind her opened, and the wind caught it and slammed it shut again with a loud bang after Eddie joined her. 'Gosh it's windy out here,' he said. 'Aren't you cold?'

Sara shoved her hair out of her face and smiled. 'No, it's lovely. My anorak's keeping me warm. I'm enjoying every minute.'

He laughed. 'We'll be there in about twenty minutes. Once we've disembarked, we'll set off straight away. I've already programmed the GPS with the address, and we should be at our destination before lunch. If you're hungry, you'd better come in now and have something to eat before they close the cafeteria.'

'Aunt Hilda gave me piles of sandwiches and a flask of tea before we left. I have more than enough for the two of us if you'd like some.'

'I've just had some sausage and chips. I'm OK now until we have our first meal in France.' He pulled the collar of his lightweight jacket up around his throat. 'You can do what you like, but I'm going back inside. It's too cold for me out here.'

Sara nodded and watched some seagulls circling above them. 'Go ahead. I'll join you in a couple of minutes.'

He tipped his chin in agreement and went back inside. Only a couple of other travellers had braved the weather to walk around the deck. Sara continued to enjoy the quiet, face the elements, and listen to the sound of the ship cutting its way through the water towards French soil.

The village, when they reached it a couple of hours later, was very pretty. They approached the hotel over an old stone bridge spanning the clear waters of a gently flowing river. Formalities were dealt with quickly and they were soon installed in their comfortable rooms. The hotel was close to where Jannet Rogard lived. It was still early afternoon when Eddie tapped on Sara's door again.

'Is everything OK?' he asked.

Sara sighed and circled the cosy room with her hand. 'Perfect!'

'Good. I'd like to visit that friend I told you about. I phoned him a couple of minutes ago and he told me to come straight over. I forgot to mention you were with me, otherwise I'd take you along. I hope you don't mind? I can't remember if it's polite to turn up with an unexpected guest in France. It's too long since I was last here. Will you be all right?'

'Don't worry about me, Eddie; I'm not a little girl. Enjoy yourself! I doubt it would be a good idea for me to come with you. You both have a lot to talk about, and I'd only be in the way. I'll go for a stroll around the village.'

'You're never in the way, but you'd probably be bored listening to two old fogeys reminiscing about the past.' He took his phone out of his pocket and waved it at her. 'I have this with me and you have my number. Phone if you need me for anything. I'll come back in a flash.'

She viewed him indulgently. 'I'm not helpless. I'll be fine. I presume you'll be back in time for dinner?'

'Yes, of course. If I don't see you before then, we'll meet at eight o'clock downstairs.'

Sara unpacked her travel bag and slipped into her cotton jacket again. A quick glance out of her window told her that the sun was out, but it was too early in the year to walk bare-armed. The GPS system in Eddie's car had taken all the stress out of working out which roads to follow. Brittany was a landscape of gently rolling hills and plains as they drove towards their destination. Sara liked what she saw; it was so different from the place where she'd grown up.

She skipped downstairs. Their hotel was the only hotel-restaurant in the village. The vestibule was empty and she ventured out onto the narrow pavement, going in no particular direction. The village was small, and there was no danger that she'd lose her way. The pavement was tarmacked here and there, but mostly it was still ancient cobblestones. Some of cottages were undoubtedly very old too. Their black-beamed frameworks criss-crossed the buildings and had white plastering between. They looked ageless. Bright red geraniums in window-boxes strained their heads towards the sun. There was also an abundance of hydrangeas in the gardens and all along the way. The bushes were a mass of blue, pink and white blooms, although blue seemed to be people's favourite.

Sara reached what she presumed was the marketplace. A stone memorial stood in the centre, surrounded by a low iron fence. Around the edge of the square she noticed a baker's shop, a butcher's, a general store selling all kinds of household necessities, a newsagent's, and also a small super-market. She walked around some wrought-iron black chairs and tables arranged higgledy-piggledy outside a kiosk in the corner. There were a couple of children's swings opposite, and a young woman was pushing a youngster back and forth and looking bored. Sara looked across at her and smiled. She decided it might be fun to see where they were going tomorrow, if it wasn't too far away. It would pass the time, and she could get to know the area in the process. She walked up to the young woman.

'Can you tell me how to get to Château Renault, please? Is it far from here?' she said in French, excited to be trying out her skill in the language.

The young woman could tell she was some kind of tourist. 'No, not far,' she replied in French. 'If you follow the road in that direction, it's about three miles. If you go via the path over there in the corner, it's only about a mile, perhaps a little more. It's easy to follow, as it passes the church and the churchyard and carries straight on to the château, then past the château to the main road at the other end. You'll be able to see the roof of the château once you pass the churchyard.'

Sara smiled and thanked her. It didn't sound complicated. She decided to try the pathway. If she was in doubt, she could always turn back. The route via the road would be more of a challenge. She set off, and soon felt relaxed and in a holiday mood as she followed the well-trodden path bordered by straggling bushes and the remnants of hedging. The air was fresh and clear, and she took deep breaths. Perhaps it was psychological, but to her Brittany felt a bit like a dream come true.

As she strode onwards, the breeze ruffled her yellow skirt. The smooth surface of the path was perfect for her flat sandals. It was evidently used often and just a few minutes later she reached the church and the churchyard. She lingered for a moment to consider the view through the entrance gates. She didn't enter, but noted straight away how different it looked in comparison to English churchyards.

She set off again and started to look

for a roof above the trees somewhere ahead of her. Coming alongside one of the fields, she noticed a man on a tractor. He was driving up and down the field, turning the soil, and leaving neat lines behind the rear of the vehicle. The tractor was chugging along loudly and the man was wearing headphones. Perhaps he could confirm that she was on the right route?

Sara halted, waved her arm and shouted, but she soon guessed he wouldn't be able to hear her above the din of the tractor's engine. She was about to move on when he must have seen her out the corner of his eye. He was coming up the field towards her now anyway, so she stayed where she was. He drove towards the edge of the field alongside the hedge and cut the engine. Leaning down, he removed the headphones.

Sara eyed him with more than general interest. He was a good-looking man and his dark eyes were intelligent and alert. He was wearing worn jeans and a navy sweatshirt that had seen better days. She guessed he was in his thirties. She considered him for a second and decided there was something different about him. Perhaps it was the compelling colour of his eyes in a sun-kissed face, the thick black hair, the firm features, or the confident set of his shoulders. If he was an ordinary farm labourer, he was a very striking one. Kelly would have instantly described him as sexy.

Sara had to bend her head right back to look up at his tanned face as he sat in the driving seat. 'Good afternoon! I'm looking for Château Renault. Am I on the right path?'

The headphones dangled from one hand. His expression was polite but with a nuance of impatience. 'Why do you want to go there? What for?'

Feeling a little irritated, she replied, 'Why do you want to know? It's nothing to do with you. I just want to know if it's further along the footpath.'

His brows straightened, and dark

irritable eyes looked out from his sun-toughened face. He considered her for a moment and then shrugged. 'Perhaps you think it's rude of me to ask what you want there, but it's very unusual to find a complete stranger wandering along this pathway to the château. You could mean trouble for the owners, and if I helped you, I could be sending an unwelcome visitor there.'

Colour rose to Sara's face. 'I don't intend to cause trouble or to intrude. I just want to know where it is and if I'm going the right way.'

The beginning of a reluctant smile touched the corners of his mouth. 'Well, it still strikes me as an odd request. The château isn't a tourist attraction. It has no special architectural highlights, and most of the gardens are overgrown and neglected. There's no earthly reason for you, a stranger, to go there, unless of course you have an invitation. And I doubt that.'

Sara was getting annoyed with him.

Her flattering thoughts of a few moments ago faded fast. 'Why don't you just carry on making holes in your field? It's absolutely immaterial to you why I want to go there, or if I have an invitation or not. Are you always so rude and unhelpful?'

There was a faint glint of humour in his eyes now, and a slight smile appeared. That only annoyed Sara more.

'For your information, I'm not digging holes, I'm ploughing.'

There was no point in fencing with him any more. Without a comment, she turned away and strode off in the direction she'd been going before she'd spotted him in the field.

She heard a soft chuckle before he called, 'OK! For your information, you're on the right path, buttercup!'

She realized his comment had been inspired by her cotton skirt, which was decorated with bright yellow flowers, and this only infuriated her more. 'Buttercup', indeed! She was tempted to respond with 'Thank you, stinging nettle,' but she didn't. It was better to ignore him.

Moments later she heard the tractor start up again. Her cheeks were bright pink and she forced herself not to look back. She carried on and soon saw the roof of a building above the tops of the trees. She wondered briefly how to react when she passed the man on the way back. Should she ignore him, or shout something rude at him over the hedge?

The path led slightly downhill, and she reached what was probably the edge of the property. It carried on around the bend, but didn't look quite as well trodden.

There was a break in the greenery, and she bent to look at the striking façade of a pink-sandstone house that blended beautifully into its surroundings. The two-storey building had neat rows of upstairs and downstairs windows framed with square lintels. The solid wood door was dark with solid iron banding, and was ajar. This was undoubtedly Château Renault. It reminded Sara of the pictures of castles in her book of fairy tales. The tractor-driver had insinuated that the gardens were overgrown, but Sara could see that someone was trying hard to cope. There was a row of neatly cut trees bordering each side of the driveway leading up from the pair of black wrought-iron gates in the distance. Some large containers, dotted here and there in strategic positions, held neatly trimmed evergreen bushes. A flowerbed meandering along the front of the house contained perennial flowers, and pink and blue hydrangeas. Sara also noted that the gravel in front of the house was clear of weeds and looked clean and raked.

A middle-aged woman came round the corner of the house. She had a long-handled hoe in her hand and was wearing jeans tucked into wellingtons, and a long-sleeved hooded jacket. She also had an old straw hat on her head, and the combination of background and person reminded Sara of pictures she'd seen in gardening magazines.

Suddenly Sara realized that this could be Jannet Rogard, and was concerned that she might be meeting her before Eddie's appointment here the following morning. The woman with the slim figure and neat brown hair could just as well be some kind of domestic help, though for some unknown reason Sara thought it unlikely. She straightened and turned away.

The colour of her skirt must have caught the other woman's attention, as she looked across in Sara's direction and shouted, 'Can I help you?'

Sara found herself grappling in her mind to find a fitting explanation for her presence at the château. The woman was coming towards her and removing her gardening gloves. Sara smiled at her and pushed the greenery aside. She held out her hand as they met.

'Good afternoon! My name is Sara Andrews. Forgive me just turning up like this, but I was curious to see the château. My friend and I have an appointment with Madame Rogard tomorrow morning, and on impulse I decided to see if I could find the château this afternoon.'

The other woman considered her for a moment, and her eyes twinkled. She looked behind Sara. 'Are you alone?'

'Yes; my friend has gone to visit someone else this afternoon. I asked someone in the village how to get to the château and she told me about this shortcut. I hope you don't mind?'

She laughed softly. 'Of course not. That path isn't a public pathway from the church onwards, because it runs across our property, but the villagers have used it for generations as a time-saver to get to the next village, or to the main road further along. Strangers seldom use it. I certainly don't mind one bit, and our predecessors didn't either. Perhaps that's one reason why the family dodged the guillotine. In those times we were very poor landowners, and not much better off than the poorest of the poor around here.'

She took Sara's hand and shook it. 'I'm Jannet Rogard. I imagine you must be thirsty if you've walked from the village. Come and have something to drink! We seldom have visitors or see strange faces here; we aren't on any tourist maps. It's nice to see someone exploring and ending up here. We have plenty of empty rooms in the château, and I plan to try to attract visitors as soon as we have the garden and house properly fixed up. I have a jug of fresh apple juice in the fridge.' Without further ado, she turned away, and Sara had little choice but to follow her.

A few minutes later she was sitting on the terrace at the back of the house. A couple of shallow steps led down to the gravel and then across grassland to a distant wood. Sara looked across to the fields in the distance.

Jannet threw her hat onto a neighbouring chair and poured them some cold apple juice. She looked at her young visitor. 'I think it would be more diplomatic to find out what you and your friend want to talk to me about tomorrow, don't you? Tell me about yourself — where you come from and what you do.'

Sara complied, and they were soon very relaxed with each other.

'I know where you come from,' Jannet said. 'I expect you realize that, don't you? You speak excellent French. Where did you learn it?'

Sara loved the compliment. 'At school, and I now go to a weekly conversation group to keep it going. My friend is in charge of the group.'

Jannet nodded. 'I can only say, well done! You must have a feeling for French. My English used to be quite good, but since my mother died I've had little opportunity to keep it fluent. It's probably very rusty now.'

'If you're planning to cater to

visitors, I think English will help. Most people speak English these days, whether they come from Japan or Russia.' Sara finished her drink and looked at her watch. 'Thank you so much for the juice; it was just what I needed. I'll head back to the village now. I have to be there in time to meet my friend when he gets back. If I'm not, he'll start to worry and call the police. I didn't tell anyone where I was going.'

Jannet nodded. 'You only have to follow the same path back, then nothing can go wrong.' They both stood up. 'I'll see you tomorrow then, Sara. I'm looking forward to meeting your friend. It was a pleasure meeting you this afternoon.'

'Me too! Thank you for being so kind. I'll see you tomorrow!'

Sara set off across the garden and through the break in the greenery. She turned once to wave to Jannet Rogard, ducked through the greenery, and then went up the slight slope. When she reached the field where the man had been busy on his tractor, the ploughing was finished and there was no one to be seen. Sara was glad. He could have mentioned the path wasn't a public one; then she would have understood his objections and might even have turned back. It was no reason for him to be so disagreeable. A simple explanation that it was on private property would have sufficed. She hoped she wouldn't meet him anywhere else again during their stay.

6

Sara told Eddie about her walk to the château as they were having their evening meal, but omitted telling him about her meeting with the man on the tractor. It would sound childish.

Eddie had enjoyed meeting his friend again, and the two men vowed they'd keep in closer touch in future. His friend was also a widower, and Eddie invited him to come to England on a visit soon. The invite was accepted and they fixed a date in the coming summer.

The meal was delicious. It wasn't the first time Sara had eaten oysters, but they'd never tasted better. It was followed by sausage on a bed of mashed potatoes, and a lemon cream pudding as dessert. During the meal they drank some Muscatel, and finally took their coffee into the small lounge just off the entrance hall. Sara thought it was good that Eddie could tell her about his own visit to his friend from his student days, as it meant she didn't need to go into much detail about her visit to Château Renault that afternoon. They both declared they'd have an early night after they finished their coffee. Sara fell asleep with an open paperback in her hands.

Next morning the sparse breakfast of milky coffee, croissants and slices of baguette with homemade jam left Eddie still feeling 'peckish'. They set off for Château Renault in plenty of time, and Sara looked at the rural countryside on the way. They passed a tourist sign pointing to a circle of menhirs, or standing stones, just outside the village. The approach to the menhirs was off the road down a narrow lane. The road to the château from the highway was much more impressive; it went past fields of vegetables and untilled meadows dotted with poppies and cornflowers.

They drove through the gates and up the long driveway.

Eddie looked around and silently nodded approval. 'It doesn't look like anyone who owns this needs Maldon Hall, does it?' he said. 'I can understand why Madame Rogard has decided to sell it. They already have enough property.'

They had barely climbed the shallow steps to the door when it opened and Jannet Rogard stood there with a welcoming smile.

Eddie stepped forward. 'Madame Rogard, I'm delighted to meet you. Sara told me she was here yesterday, and she said you were very kind and hospitable.'

'Good morning, Mr Protheroe. Hello, Sara! Won't you both come in? We'll go into the sitting room — it's through that door there in the corner. It looks out onto the back of the house. I remember enough of English tradition to know you might like a cup of tea.'

The other two followed her and entered the comfortable sitting room. It was elegant in its proportions, and there were some beautiful pieces of old furniture; but the carpet was a little threadbare, and the brocade curtains were sun-bleached and needed to be replaced. There was a dark figure standing in one of the window's long alcoves.

'This is my son, Dominique — or Nick, as he prefers to be called,' said Jannet. 'I presume your visit has to do with Maldon House, and if that is so I thought it was a good idea for Nick to be here. He knows what's going on.'

Eddie nodded. 'Of course. That's perfectly understandable. Morning, Nick! I hope I can call you Nick? I'm Eddie Protheroe, and this is a friend of mine, Sara Andrews.'

The man stepped out of the shadows and held out his hand to Eddie. Sara saw with a shock that it was the man on the tractor from yesterday. He looked completely different this morning. He was at ease with himself in a stylish tweed jacket that skimmed his figure, a white shirt and beige trousers. His black hair was a little tousled, and he gave her an amused nod. He had an advantage over her because he'd probably guessed who she was yesterday, and knew they would meet again this morning.

Eddie explained, 'We're here because Sara and I both live in near Maldon, and what happens to it effects everyone who lives in the village. We were asked to represent them and come to ask you about your future plans for the place. People are afraid that the plot Maldon House is on will be sliced up and sold off without regard to how the village will look afterwards.'

Sara stared at Nick, her mouth was dry. Neither of them had acknowledged the other or indicated that they'd already met, so when Jannet gestured them to nearby chairs, everyone sat down. Sara studied the faded pattern on the carpet for a moment and then concentrated on Jannet's voice.

As she was about to answer, Eddie said, 'Before we go any further, I have to mention that we've met before, Jannet.'

She looked surprised. 'Have we? When? Where?'

'At Maldon House. You came on a visit once with your mother and we played in the garden. You, me and several other children from the village.'

'Did we?' She studied him more carefully. 'Is it really you, Eddie?' He nodded and smiled. 'You seemed familiar, but I thought it was merely my imagination. A lot of water has flowed under the bridge since those days. We've all changed, haven't we?' She laughed. 'What a lovely surprise.'

Eddie hastened to say, 'You haven't changed a bit. I'd have recognized you anywhere.'

'Oh, don't flatter me, Eddie! How long ago was it? Forty years? No, it must be even longer. You had blond hair in those days, and you're much taller than you were then, but you still have the same mischievous, energetic look. Are you married? Children?'

'I was, but my wife died a couple of years ago.' She nodded in silent sympathy. 'I have two children, a boy and a girl.'

Nick coughed in the background as Jannet and Eddie looked at each other silently. The interruption brought their attention back to the present. Jannet leaned forward and began to pour them tea from a laden tray on a side-table, then offered some homemade cake. Eddie accepted both gratefully. Sara refused the cake but accepted the tea. Her throat felt like sandpaper. Jannet handed Nick a cup, and he continued to stand to one side, drinking now and then.

Jannet commented, 'I've heard noth ing about building plots, Eddie. Naturally I discussed the situation with Nick and talked to the solicitor who's tying up my uncle's estate. We decided the best thing would be to give the solicitor instructions to try to sell Maldon House in one piece if possible. Nick says he has no interest in it, and I'm based here in France too, so there's no point in us keeping it. We couldn't afford long-distance upkeep, even if we wanted to.'

Eddie nodded. 'Yes, I understand. May I ask if it's officially up for sale yet?'

Nick's cup clattered on his saucer and he joined in. 'The lawyers intended to use a reliable estate agent and tell them to try to sell it as soon as possible. If it doesn't sell as a single unit, my mother will be forced to think about splitting it up into smaller plots to get rid of it that way. I've seen the plans of the house and the grounds. It's quite a lot of land. Not many people can afford to buy something that size these days. The prospect of finding a single buyer isn't very good.'

Sara felt it was time for her to join in the discussion. 'There are people with plenty of money who might be interested. Arabian sheiks, Russian oil billionaires, pop stars — they all have more money than sense, and might want to show a residence in the English countryside off to the rest of the world.'

Nick turned in her direction. 'And you wouldn't mind that? You prefer to have pop stars invading your village rather than letting someone build family homes? I don't know what your village is like, but it would probably be better for the community to have houses with families than owners who are never there, and don't care about the village or its inhabitants.'

Colour flooded her cheeks and her brown eyes flashed. She glowered at him. 'It's easy for you to say that, since you don't have to live with the consequences. How would you like someone building houses on one of the fields overlooking your home?'

The line of his mouth tightened a fraction and he gave her a stiff smile. 'Not much, but sometimes you have to accept the inevitable.'

Sara's tone was civil in spite of the anger she felt. 'But it *isn't* inevitable. That's why we're here. We hoped we could persuade your mother to listen to our case and take our side.'

He replied sharply, 'It's up to my mother how much she wants to get involved. She's inherited the place, not the villagers.'

Jannet lifted her hands. 'Steady on, you two. Nothing has been decided yet, and the solicitors need my permission to close any deal, so I'll be able to keep an eye on things. I'm glad that Sara and Eddie came to see us. To be honest, when I first heard, I thought the best thing to do would be to sell fast, but I see that the situation is more complicated than that. I promise I'll try to find the best solution for everyone concerned.'

Eddie nodded. 'That's all that we can expect. Maldon House is yours, and naturally you're entitled to do what you like with it; but we wanted you to know that the villagers are afraid that the whole atmosphere will change if the plot is cut up into bits and pieces. The house was always an important focal point. It's a symbol of continuity and tradition. We can't imagine how it will be if builders put up a bunch of modern houses in inappropriate spots.'

Nick was looking out of the window again. Sara stared determinedly at a cherry-wood cabinet containing some old leather-bound books. Jannet and Eddie talked on, and she heard Eddie telling her about the information he'd gathered.

Finally Jannet said, 'I'll remember what you told us, Eddie. At present I can only say that we're going to sell Maldon House, and we hope to find the best solution for us and for the community. Leave it with me. Give me your home number, and I'll be in touch as soon as I've thought things over and talked to the lawyers again. My uncle trusted them, and they handled his legal affairs all his life. Perhaps they can steer the estate agent in a direction that will suit us all.' She looked at her son. 'Nick, why don't you show Sara around? It will give Eddie and me a chance to talk about old times.'

Stiffly he put his cup on a nearby table and said, 'Gladly!' He walked towards the door and opened it. Sara had little choice but to put her own cup down and follow him. She wished could say that she didn't need a guided tour. Nick gave her an encouraging smile before he grabbed another slice of cake and led the way out of the room.

Sara trailed after him; and when they were outside, he suddenly remembered his manners and waited for her to catch up. 'What would you like to see?' he asked.

She noticed his set face and fixed eyes. 'I don't care. Whatever you think will fill in the appropriate amount of time.'

'Right! I'll show you the barn with my machinery.'

'Fascinating, I'm sure!'

He led the way and she followed him inside, where she saw an impressive array of large machines that were clearly in regular use on the farm. 'What do you use it all for?'

'Ploughing, seed-drilling, slurry-spreading, harvesting the vegetables we grow, hay-turning, hay-baling, et cetera. We don't need much hay ourselves, so we sell it to some local dairy farmers.'

The machinery looked well cared for, but it was foreign to Sara, and she felt a little intimidated by it. She listened politely as Nick pointed out how some of the machines functioned. He suddenly turned to her and ran his hand down his face. 'Look — this is stupid, isn't it? I admit I was rather rude yesterday. I only intended to have a bit of fun, but you got so het up that it only encouraged me to carry on. Your face was a picture.' He grinned. 'You hurried off before I could straighten things out again. Let's pretend that it never happened.'

81

Sara shrugged and nervously moistened her dry lips. 'OK.'

He discarded his jacket and threw it over his arm. 'You know what I do. I drive a tractor around the fields and open my mouth too much sometimes. What do you do?'

She bit her lip and stifled a grin. 'I'm a librarian, and sometimes I ask strange people annoying questions.'

An easy smile played at the corners of his mouth and she relaxed. 'Come on!' He turned on his heel and strode towards the door. 'I'll show you my mother's favourite spot. She's made a rose garden, and she adores it.'

'Sounds a lot more interesting to me. Lead the way!'

They strolled side by side, and he told her a little about the history of the château and also about a circle of menhirs in one of the distant fields. He pointed towards them. They were tiny black dots from where they were standing. 'There's nowhere else in the world where you'll find as many as in

Brittany. No one knows why they were erected. Speculation has gone on for centuries.'

Sara nodded. 'I read somewhere that experts thought they were burial sites of chiefs or kings, while others say they were meeting places where ceremonial or religious acts of some kind took place at certain times of the year.'

'There are also countless folk tales connected to these circles and other megalithic monuments. Probably no one will ever know the real truth.'

They'd reached a big hollowed-out square of ground that wasn't immediately visible until you were up close. Below it was a mass of rose bushes. Some steps led down to paved pathways that criss-crossed the area. The flower-beds were full of roses in bud, but not yet in bloom.

Sara followed Nick down the steps and stood looking around. 'Wow! Your mother did this? She must have muscles like Hercules!' He laughed, and the glow of his smile warmed something inside her.

'She wanted roses,' he said, 'but the wind causes havoc sometimes. She persuaded me to bulldoze a hole and spread suitable earth for planting. Once I'd done that and secured the sides, I left her to it. That was two or three years ago. As you see, the banking is now nicely covered in grass, and I made the steps and the pathways last winter. Her rose bushes are strong and doing well. I don't share her passion for all this gardening — I have enough to do on the estate, but last year this was a mass of colour, and the scent was unbelievable.'

'The roses must've cost a fortune. It's a large plot of ground.'

'She already had some bushes in other places — a group here and another group there, as she tried to find somewhere suited to growing them. She also asked for cuttings from friends, and it was never a problem deciding what to give her as a present for birthdays or Christmas! The fact that they're in this dip in the ground protects them from any strong wind, and they still get lots of sunshine. Our climate is fairly mild — and hey presto, we have healthy, strong roses down here that smell like a perfume shop when they bloom.'

'I've never seen anything quite like it,' Sara enthused. 'The idea is great, but it's a lot of work. When did you find time to help her? You have a farm to run.'

'In winter, when there wasn't so much to do. She spends hours down here caring for them, deadheading them in the summer, and pruning them back in the autumn. She worships them. She'd love to concentrate on gardening every day, but she also takes care of the house and helps me with office work.'

They were interrupted when a young woman appeared at the top of the steps. She was silhouetted against the sun, and at first Sara couldn't see her face properly.

'Dominique, your mother told me

you were showing a guest round. I've been searching for you.'

Nick turned and went back up the steps. Sara followed. The girl kissed his cheeks French fashion, and he turned to Sara. As he introduced her, however, his voice trailed off as he didn't know he surname. She helped him with the additional 'Andrews'.

'Sara Andrews!' he echoed. 'I was showing her my pride and joy, all the machinery in the barn, and she wasn't impressed, so I brought her here to admire my mother's rose garden. Sara, this is Madeleine. She's a neighbour and a long-standing friend of mine and my family's.'

Sara smiled and said, 'Hello, pleased to meet you.'

Madeleine was a little shorter than Sara. She was dressed quite smartly in a floral summer dress and denim jacket. Her dark hair swung like a straight curtain to her shoulders, and she had an attractive face. She smiled back and said, 'Hello.'

'I meant to ask — ' Nick said to Sara ' — how come you speak such good French?'

'One of my main subjects in the upper form. I've always loved French and it was never a chore. Perhaps I was French in a previous lifetime.' From the way Madeleine's glance flitted constantly in Nick's direction, Sara decided it was time to leave them. 'I'll stroll around on my own now, Nick. There's no need for you to waste your time. I'll see you in the house later.'

He lifted his hand as a sign of emerging protest, but Madeleine grabbed him and proceeded to pull him towards the barn. 'Dominique, I need your help. I came over on my bike and the chain has come off.'

He looked at Sara and offered her a sudden arresting smile before he shrugged his shoulders and was dragged away in the opposite direction.

7

Sara avoided the area around the outbuildings, where she presumed she'd find Nick with Madeleine. She liked what she saw of the house and its grounds. There was a lot of work still to be done to tame some of the surrounding garden and peripheral greenery, but she could already imagine how it would look when Jannet had more time to concentrate on doing the thing she loved most of all, gardening. She'd gradually restore the estate to the way it had looked in its heyday, though it was clear she'd need help to do some of the manual jobs. Nick was tied up in estate work, but perhaps the money from the inheritance would help there. She'd be able to employ a full-time help in the house too.

When Sara went indoors again, Eddie and Jannet were still sitting where she'd left them, lost in memories of Maldon House and all that had happened to them since they'd last met. She didn't like interrupting them, as they seemed so comfortable with each other, but she wondered if she and Eddie might be outstaying their welcome. Eddie was lost in his memories, but Jannet had a lot to do. Perhaps she was just too polite to say so.

They both looked up when she came in. Eddie was a little startled when he checked his watch. 'Good lord! Is it really gone twelve already?' He stood up. 'It's been such pleasure to meet you again, Jannet.'

She stood up too. 'Must you go? Stay and have lunch with me. Nick usually never bothers; he's always busy and doesn't generally interrupt what he's doing during the day. Usually he just takes sandwiches with him. He eats like horse in the evening, though.'

Eddie took her shoulders and kissed her French style, then held her at arm's length. 'Thank you, my dear, but we've been here long enough. On our way here, Sara noticed a sign pointing to a menhir circle down one of the side roads. We're going to play at being tourists.'

Jannet smiled softly. 'I know the one you mean. It's nothing special, I'm afraid.'

Eddie tilted his head and smiled. 'Well we'll take a look anyway, and then we'll probably head back to the hotel. I'm extremely grateful that you'll keep our concerns in mind when you decide what to do with Maldon House. That's all we can ask of you.'

'I will, I promise! Are you sure you won't stay for lunch?' He shook his head. 'Well I hope you have a safe journey home. When are you leaving?'

'Sara has to be back at work on Monday morning. I've booked a passage for seven p.m. on Sunday. We should be back in the village by ten to ten-thirty.'

'So you have this afternoon and tomorrow morning free?'

He nodded. 'We won't be bored. It's not far from here to the coast. I'd like to show Sara some of Brittany's beautiful coastline before we leave.'

Jannet came with them to the door. Eddie said, 'Our best wishes to Nick. And I hope you'll take care of yourself, and not overdo things.' He gestured towards the gardens. 'I can tell you love your garden. But if you also have this house to look after, as well as doing office work for Nick, you'll stretch yourself too far one day.'

She laughed softly. 'Thanks, but don't worry. Nick keeps his eye on me and nags constantly too. But I refuse to be idle when Nick is busy day and night. Gardening is not a chore, Eddie. I love it. Looking after the house and keeping an eye on the estate work are more like chores, but someone has to do them.'

Eddie looked at her again before he opened the car door for Sara and got into the driving seat. Jannet stood in the doorway watching until they disappeared down the driveway.

Sara broke the silence and said, 'I like her. She's very down-to-earth and level-headed. She wasn't obliged to listen to us, but she understood why we wanted to explain our point of view.'

Eddie's hands gripped the steering wheel tightly. 'Yes, she always was a nice person; time hasn't changed that at all. Now, let's go and look at this circle. We can go on to the next town after that, if you like, to have a look round.'

'That sounds lovely. Are you sure you don't want to go back for an afternoon nap?'

He glanced across at her quickly. 'Sara! I'm not in my dotage. I won't pretend I never have forty winks when I get the chance, but I don't intend to waste time sleeping when I'm in Brittany for the weekend.'

It was a pleasant afternoon. The circle of stones was less impressive than Sara expected, but perhaps she was hoping for something rather more extraordinary. The spot was in a clearing in the forest. Sunlight cut through the greenery of the surrounding trees and fell on the ground where the stones stood. The little hollow was thick with brown needles and moss. Sara didn't think that the circle had been in the middle of trees in ancient times, but anything was possible, and no one knew the rhyme or reason behind the building of the prehistoric stone circle. She recalled her brief conversation with Nick about them. One or two of the upright stones had fallen over, and you needed a vivid imagination to visualise how it had once looked. There was a plastic sign with a picture on a rotting post, and that helped. They still agreed it was an interesting spot; and the complete silence, apart from the call of an occasional bird in the undergrowth, added to the atmosphere.

Their visit to the nearby market town was noisier, and quite enjoyable. They took their time viewing the place and the people as they drifted through the indoor area and were confronted with a large choice of vegetables, cheeses, and fresh fish. Neither of them recognized some of the foods on offer. There was also a good variety of fruit. Everything looked locally produced and probably tasted wonderful. Sara bought a piece of local cheese that smelt fantastic to take back for Aunt Hilda. They stopped at a pavement café for an apple crêpe with whipped cream. Eddie ate two with his milky coffee.

Eventually they drove back to the hotel, and after a brief spell to freshen up they enjoyed yet another delicious meal in the small dining room. They agreed on a constitutional walk around the village afterwards and stopped on the old stone bridge for a short while, watching the clear waters bubbling over the pebbles beneath them in the shallow river. Darkness was descending fast by the time they reached the hotel once more. They were about to climb the stairs to their rooms when the owner hurried in.

'Monsieur Protheroe,' he said, 'Madame Rogard telephoned when you were out and asked me to tell you to phone her when you got back. She said she would wait up until you called, however late it was.'

Eddie looked at his watch. 'I wonder what she wants. Do you have her number, please?'

The man fumbled in his pocket and handed him a piece of crumpled paper, then pointed to the telephone on the reception desk. 'Help yourself, monsieur.' Having done his duty, he left them and disappeared into the private part of the hotel.

Eddie was puzzled, but hurriedly dial the number. 'Yes, hello Jannet. You wanted to talk to me?' He listened for a moment or two, nodding his head now and then. 'Right! That's kind of you both. We'll see you tomorrow morning then, round nine-thirty. Bye!'

'What was that about?' Sara asked.

'Jannet and Nick have offered to take

us to the coast tomorrow. Nick was going there anyway. Apparently he sails regularly, and Jannet thought it might be interesting for us to go with them and see some of the local coastline. It isn't far. The coast is close even if you live inland.'

Sara's heart skipped a beat. She couldn't help but look forward to the prospect of seeing Nick again, and his mother of course. There was something about him that piqued her curiosity and heightened her awareness. She wouldn't see him again after tomorrow, but she still looked forward to it. She liked Jannet too.

'That's kind of them,' Sara said to Eddie. 'Are they coming to pick us up, or will we follow them in your car?'

'We're booking out tomorrow anyway. If we pack our bags and settle our bill straight after breakfast, Jannet suggested we drive there, leave our car and go with them. She promises we'll be back in plenty of time to drive to the ferry.'

8

'Where are we going?' Eddie asked. He was sitting next to Nick in the front passenger seat.

'We're on the road between Brest and Roscoff, heading for Le Folgoet. From there, it's fifteen miles west to a place called l'Aber-Wrac'h. The coastline is rugged. It used to be notorious for shipwrecks, but the sea cuts into l'Aber-Wrac'h, and it also has some magnificent sheltered beaches.'

'That sounds almost Welsh — l'Aber-Wrac'h — doesn't it?' Sara said.

'Do you know any Welsh?' Jannet asked. 'Wales and Brittany have languages from the same source.'

'No, but my father was Welsh, and I've always been interested in the language.'

'Really? Where does your mother come from? Where do they live?'

'They're both dead,' Sara answered. 'I can't remember my father, and my mother was killed in a car accident when I was six. I grew up with an aunt, my mother's sister.'

'Oh how awful! What about your Welsh relatives?'

The engine purred efficiently and Sara shrugged. 'I don't know. Whenever I used to ask my aunt about them, she'd close up like a clam. I gave up trying.'

'Well, you're old enough now to make your own enquiries, aren't you?' Jannet said. 'I think I'd want to know more.'

'You're right. I haven't thought about it for a while.'

Eddie added, 'The woman is a pain in the neck.'

Sara laughed. 'Don't start again, Eddie! She took me in. If she'd refused, I could've ended up in an orphanage, and that would've been harder. She's done her best.'

'That doesn't explain why she

became the bane of your existence. It's a wonder that you turned out so well.'

Jannet patted her hand. 'Yes, that's very true. I can tell that already.'

Sara looked up and met Nick's eyes in the rear mirror. She could see unwritten sympathy there, but she didn't want anyone's pity or compassion. She looked down quickly and then out the side window.

The conversation moved on to comments about places they were passing through. Jannet sometimes added some colourful local tales. Brittany seemed to be a land of myths and legends. It suited Sara down to the ground. She loved make-believe and fantasy.

They drove into the small port. Nick parked the jeep close to the marina, where numerous boats were bobbing on the water, waiting for the arrival of their owners.

Jannet explained, 'Nick is leaving us to go sailing with his friend André. They'll be back in plenty of time to drive us home again.'

Sara felt a tinge of disappointment. She was hoping to spend more time with him. Eddie nodded understandingly.

Nick asked her, 'Can you sail? You could come with us.'

She shook her head. 'No, I can't. I'd only be a liability. Enjoy yourself.'

'Nick!' A man came hurrying towards them. He was shorter than Nick, with a muscular body and dark hair. His smile split his face in two, and he had laughing green eyes. He greeted the others and gave Sara a close appraisal before he introduced himself. 'André, Mademoiselle Sara!' And he kissed her French fashion.

Nick stood aside and watched his friend indulgently, then slapped him on the shoulder. 'Stop flirting. We're here to sail. Come on — let's get going and make the most of the day!'

André tilted his head to one side and asked hopefully, 'And Sara? Isn't she coming?'

She laughed. 'No, I'm not.'

'What a pity! Still, duty calls I suppose. I hope to see you later, Sara.' The two men turned away and headed towards the marina.

Eddie asked, 'Does Nick own a boat?'

'No,' replied Jannet. 'André, Nick and another friend of theirs bought one between them a couple of years ago. Nick's uncle left him a small legacy, and Nick was very reluctant to spend the money that way, but I'm so glad I encouraged him to. He loves sailing, and it gets him away from the estate. It does him a world of good. So what would you two like to do? Shall we go for a walk and come back to have a meal later?'

Sara and Eddie agreed, and they went walking. It was quieter everywhere; much quieter than Sara expected. She thought sheltered beaches like these would be busy, but tourism hadn't completely taken over yet, and there was a very relaxing atmosphere. They sat down on a conveniently placed bench now and then.

Once, when Eddie went off to look at an antique car parked on the side of the road and chat to its owner, Sara sighed. 'These past few days have made me determined to spend my next holiday in France this summer. I'd love to stay for a longer period. I went to the Provence with the school once, and I liked that, but it was full of tourists. Brittany isn't so swamped.'

'No it isn't,' Jannet agreed. 'It's not as sunny as the south of the country, but it's milder than a lot of people expect. If you want to come back, get in touch.' She pointed to some bright wildflowers growing nearby. 'Aren't they pretty?'

The hidden invitation was tempting, but Sara thought Jannet might only feel obliged to extend it to her. She was that kind of person. 'You love flowers, don't you?' she said to the older woman. 'Most people don't give wildflowers more than a passing glance. Some don't even see them at all.'

Jannet laughed. 'Yes, but I don't just love just cultivated flowers. I'm interested in anything to do with plants and trees. My mother was the same, and she started taming the garden until the family ran out of money. I hope I'm not boring you with my hobby?'

'Of course not.'

'I find myself constantly thinking up new plans for the garden. I can imagine lots of new ideas. My present problem is how to blend the edge of our actual garden into the fields beyond without making obvious boundaries like fences or hedging. I'd like a softer, less obvious verge of some kind.'

Sara shifted. 'I don't know much about gardening, but what about a ha-ha?'

'What's a ha-ha?'

'You must have heard of them, or seen one. I have a feeling they came from France — or was it China? As far as I can recall, it's a wide ditch between the cultivated part of the garden and the landscape beyond. They were popular because they kept animals and unwanted guests away from grand houses, but they didn't interrupt the view. From the house you couldn't see the transition; it looked like the garden blended into the countryside beyond. A lot of famous landscape gardeners used them. They were an attempt to make the gardens and parklands of large houses blend naturally with their surroundings. A bit like your sunken rose garden, only running the length of the end of your garden.'

'Hmm! It rings a bell but I can't say I've seen one. It definitely sounds better than using hedges, fences or rows of trees. Less maintenance in the long run too.'

'I think some had walls at the bottom, out of sight, but that isn't obligatory. They were probably a lot of work to make, especially if it was large parkland. I'll see if I can find any pictures and information about them when I get back. I'll send it to you, if you like.'

'Please do; I'll be interested. I'll have to hide it from Nick, though. He'll have a heart attack! He's only just finished helping me with the rose garden.'

They walked for a while and admired the rough coastline and fantastic sandy beaches. Gradually they all admitted they were getting hungry. Sara shared a bar of chocolate with the others and they turned back to the marina. They found the two friends already sitting on the stone terrace outside the restaurant, waiting for them.

André nudged Nick. 'See what I mean? The little English girl has a curvy figure and her hair is like burnt copper. She's pretty too. It's a pity she won't be staying, otherwise I'd try my luck.'

Nick laughed and was thoughtful. Yes, she was attractive. Her brown eyes were soft and appealing. He'd always had a weakness for brown eyes.

When the others reached them, Jannet exclaimed, 'This is a surprise! I thought you'd be out until late this afternoon?'

'We decided to cut it short today,' André said. 'The wind is too blustery and changeable. We thought it'd be more enjoyable to have lunch with our English friends.'

The men had already booked a table by the window. The view over the marina, the food, the company, and the weather outside made it a day to remember.

Eddie slipped out to pay the bill, and Nick and Jannet protested when they found out. After finishing their coffee and saying farewell to André, with lots of kisses and flattery, they set off for Château Renault again. Sara vowed to make Eddie let her repay him for part of the meal. She'd already had to insist on paying her own bill at the hotel that morning.

They arrived at the château in plenty of time, and Jannet insisted they have a cup of tea before they set out for the ferry. When it was finally time to go,

Sara felt quite nostalgic. It was as if she'd known Jannet forever, and she also wished she'd had more time to get to know Nick properly.

They all came to the top of the steps, and Jannet kissed Sara's cheek. 'I hope to see you again,' she said. 'Have a safe journey home.'

'Thank you — and thanks for all your kindness and hospitality.' Sara held out her hand to Nick. 'Goodbye, Nick. Thanks for not throwing us out on our ears!'

Nick took her hand and held it a moment too long, before he reached out and kissed her French fashion on her cheeks too. Sara was flustered, but it was a perfect end to a very enjoyable weekend. While Jannet and Eddie were busy with their own goodbyes, Nick added quietly. 'Bye, buttercup. Who knows, perhaps we'll meet again one day.'

She managed a tremulous smile. 'There you go again — reminding me of what I wanted to forget.'

He grinned and her heart missed a beat. 'I prefer to remember it. Take care of yourself!'

'I will. You too!' Sara went towards the car and was glad to be facing away from Nick and able to hide her expression.

The trip back across the Channel was smooth and uneventful, and they both agreed that the journey had been well worth the effort.

9

Kelly burst into the library just as Sara was about to lock up for the day. 'Good, I caught you! I'm going out later on, but I have to tell you about my weekend, and hear how your trip with Eddie went.' She waited impatiently while Sara grabbed her jacket. After turning off the lights, Sara ushered Kelly back out of the door and locked it. They set off down the street.

A few impatient steps later, Kelly sighed. 'I think I'm in love!'

Sara stopped in her tracks. 'What?' Kelly had never said she was even a little bit in love with someone before, not as long as Sara had known her. The expression on her friend's face was unfamiliar, and there was a glow about her.

Kelly hesitated and stared at her. 'I

know — it's mad, isn't it? I can't explain it myself either. I just know Mark is the one. I feel that I've known him forever.'

Sara lifted her eyebrows. 'And what about him? Do you think he feels the same?'

'I'm not sure. He said he likes me, but that could mean anything.'

'Kelly, just please be careful. Don't expect too much of him too soon. Maybe he doesn't feel the same way. You'll get hurt if he gets bored and calls it a day. Be grateful that he likes you, and take it from there. Don't put pressure on him.'

Kelly put her hands on her hips. 'I'm not stupid. No way would I force him into anything. I'm not going to run into his arms and demand a white wedding. I just had to tell someone how I felt, and you're the first person I thought of.'

Sara hugged her. 'And . . . how does it feel?'

'It's hard to put into words,' Kelly

sighed happily. 'I thought he was interesting that evening he came to talk in the parish hall. When we spent the weekend together, I decided he wasn't only attractive and interesting, but there was something about him that was so refreshingly different too. It's like I've known him all my life. He's fun to be with, he's protective, and he makes me feel good. We're going out again this evening to the cinema. I can't wait to see him again.'

Sara hoped her friend wouldn't be disappointed. She found herself drawing a comparison to what she'd felt about Nick, but she wasn't in love with him. She was just interested.

Eventually Kelly remembered to ask, 'What about your weekend? Did it work out OK?' She looked briefly at her watch as she did so.

Sara smiled. 'Yes, it was fine. Go on, off you go! Go get home and get yourself prettied up for Mark. We can talk about it another time.'

Kelly gave her a peck on the cheek.

'You're a gem. I'll phone soon, promise.'

'Have a nice time!'

Kelly hurried off down the road, waving her hand in reply.

* * *

The following week, Eddie came into the library to see Sara. 'Jannet is coming,' he said with a huge smile. 'She said she wanted to talk to the lawyers and take a look around Maldon House to see if she wanted to keep anything before they start to take prospective buyers on viewings.'

'Are there any prospective buyers?' Sara said.

'Your guess is as good as mine. I didn't ask her.'

'Where's she staying?'

'Ah! I invited her to stay with me, and she accepted.'

'Oh, Eddie! What will your daily help say? And what about others in the village?' Sara laughed softly.

'I know, I know! Mary will give me looks and ask awkward questions, but I don't care.'

'That's the spirit. Well if you need any help from me, just ask.'

'Will you come round and check my guest room before she arrives? Mary keeps everything ship-shape and Bristol fashion, but I want it to be perfect for Jannet. You can tell me if I should buy something or change anything before she arrives.'

'You have a lovely cottage and you keep it very neat and tidy. Jannet is more likely to look at your garden than at the contents of your home!'

'Gosh! Yes, you're right there. I'd better have a go at completely banishing the weeds and getting the lawn out the back into tip-top condition.' He looked at his watch. 'I just have time to go to B&Q for some fertilizer.'

Sara laughed. 'Off you go, then. I look forward to seeing her again. And I'd like to take her to see a stately home when she's here, or rather I'd like to show her round one of the stately homes with a famous garden. Now that I've passed my driving test, I can borrow Aunt Hilda's car for the day. I think Jannet would enjoy that.'

Eddie nodded. 'I'm sure she would. We must share a meal together one evening. It would have to be something simple that I can manage. A barbeque, maybe.'

★ ★ ★

Jannet sat opposite Sara in a small café near the stately home and gardens they'd been visiting, drinking coffee and savouring a piece of iced fruitcake.

'So, what do you think? Did you like the house?' Sara asked her.

'It's absolutely fantastic. Thank you so much for bringing me, Sara. What I like most of all is that the garden is so natural. It's beautiful without having masses of flowers everywhere. The trees, the shrubs, and the way everything has been planned is perfect.

114

Wherever you stand, the views are fantastic.' She took a sip of her coffee. 'Oh, by the way, thank you for the gardening book and the pictures of ha-has. It was lovely. I was going to write to you, but then my lawyers suggested I come over in person to sign some papers and discuss the situation. It was very kind of you to remember.'

Sara brushed her thanks aside. 'My pleasure!'

'It was very enlightening to actually see a real ha-ha today. I'm seriously thinking of using the idea for my garden, when and if I can afford it.'

'Perhaps you'll be able to when you sell Maldon House. Any buyers yet?'

'No definite offers, but there are enquiries. I told them to try to sell it as is stands. If not, we'll have to decide where to go from there.'

'And Eddie told me you wanted to visit Maldon House again. Have you been there yet? Was it depressing? You must have thought about the time your mother was alive when you visited Mr Harper.'

'Yes, it was sad in a way, but I'm glad I've seen it again. I went round it with Eddie and I put stickers on things that I'd like to keep. There are some lovely bits and pieces. It'd be a shame to lose so much family furniture. Once we've renovated the château, I'd like to put it in the various rooms. I imagine that from the number of things I marked, it will mean a full removal van. Eddie has offered to organize the transport.' She looked at Sara contemplatively. 'If you need some furniture, just tell me and I'll get the lawyer to give you the key.'

Sara smiled at her. 'Thanks, but I have nowhere to store anything. If I already had my own flat, I might have been interested.'

'Pity! Have you tried to find out anything more about your Welsh relatives yet?'

'No, but I fully intend to.'

'And what about France? Have you booked your holiday yet? You said you were thinking of spending a couple of weeks next time you come.'

'I'd like to, but I haven't sorted out with my boss yet when I can take my holiday time. I'd like to take three or four weeks together, but that's unusual. People usually take their holidays in bits and pieces.'

'Well, write and tell me if you're near us, or if you're just passing on the way there or back. You must come and see us if you do.'

'Perhaps. I'm going to buy my own car. I was intending to save for a flat, but I've changed my mind. I still want my own flat, but I'll enjoy having my own car more at the moment. It'll give me more freedom.'

'What does your aunt think about the idea of you leaving her?'

'She understands, but she keeps warning me about all the dangers. She didn't say so, but I think it's partly because she'd miss me.'

'She's bound to, but you ought to live your own life. It's a pity you don't have a flat. You could have filled it with furniture from Maldon House. Nick ought to be living in his own flat, but the position is slightly different because he took over the estate unexpectedly, and someone has to cook and take care of things so that he can concentrate on the work. That will change if he gets married, and then we'll need to split the house in some way. Luckily we've always got on, but I don't think it's a good idea for parents-in-law to be involved in their children's daily lives. Everyone needs their own space.'

Hesitatingly, Sara asked, 'How is he?'

Jannet smiled. 'Fine. I left the freezer full of pre-prepared meals, and I expect Madeleine will keep an eye on him.'

'Are Madeleine and Nick . . . ' Sara paused.

Jannet shook her head. 'I don't think so. I keep hinting about getting married, but Nick brushes it aside. He's known Madeleine all his life. In a way it would make everything easier, because she comes from a farming background;

but to spend the rest of your life with someone, you have to love them. I drop hints, but my son knows what he's doing. He brought a couple of girls home for the weekend now and then when he was still at agricultural college, but it came to nothing.'

Sara wrung her hands under the table. 'From what I saw of Nick, I think he'll decide on his own future. He won't appreciate any interference.'

Jannet's eyebrows lifted, and she looked at Sara for a second before she asked, 'Can we go to the souvenir shop before we leave? I'd like to get some postcards and see if they have any interesting gardening books.'

* * *

Eddie started to organize the moving of the furniture for Jannet, and they continued to write to each other regularly after the Frenchwoman returned home. Sara got permission to take four weeks of holiday time, and

Kelly was still going out with Mark.

No one wanted to buy Maldon House as it stood. The protest committee didn't have anything definite to protest about yet, but they all presumed the selling process would now move on to the stage of trying to sell it in smaller portions. Eddie was caught between a rock and a hard place. On the one hand, he didn't want to spoil his growing friendship with Jannet; but on the other, he wanted to prevent Maldon House from being sacrificed to the highest bidder just to build houses where no one wanted them to be built.

Summer arrived, and the days were brighter and often sunny. Sara was looking forward to leaving for France in a week's time, and had decided to cross the Channel and drive from place to place without a set plan. She felt quite adventurous. Perhaps places would be booked out, but at least she had her own car, and it wouldn't matter if she carried on until she found somewhere to stay. She'd have to keep an eye on her purse, but she was used to doing that.

Eddie hurried into the library one morning. Sara smiled at him and said, 'Morning, Eddie!'

'Morning, my dear.' He looked around. 'Are you busy?'

'No. As you see, the library is not exactly teeming with borrowers this morning.'

'You're going on holiday at the beginning of next week, aren't you?'

'Yes.'

'And you haven't made any definite plans to go anywhere yet?'

'No.'

'Good. Jannet just phoned. Apparently she tripped and broke her leg last week. Nick is driving her crazy because he keeps fussing around and telling her what she can and can't do.'

'And?'

'She wondered if you'd come and stay with them for a while. She wants you to enjoy yourself and feel free to see Brittany; but if you stayed with them,

121

she thinks Nick would leave her in peace if he knew someone else was keeping an eye on her while he's busy on the estate. It would mean he could concentrate on work and wouldn't keep rushing back to check on her. She hates that.'

'Isn't there anyone else who'd help?' Sara's heartbeat quickened as she thought about returning to Château Renault, but she tried to be sensible. 'What about that girl I met there? Madeleine, their neighbour's daughter.'

'I don't think I met her, did I? Jannet has taken a shine to you and is convinced you'd be perfect and wouldn't treat her like an invalid. I don't know why she won't accept anyone else, but I do understand why she likes you.'

'Wow!' Sara pushed her hair off her face. She was glad of a moment's delay when a reader came up to get her books registered. Then, looking up at Eddie, she declared, 'I was planning to just travel around and stop where I liked. I wasn't thinking of staying exclusively in Brittany.'

He shrugged. 'It's up to you. I know it means you wouldn't see as much of France as you hoped to, but on the other hand you'd be in Brittany long enough to get a real feel for that part of France and the people who live there. I'm not sure how long Jannet's leg has already been in plaster. The healing process usually takes six weeks or thereabouts, doesn't it? You might be able to go somewhere else for the last week or two if she's already been in plaster for a while.'

'What about Nick? Does he approve?'

Eddie laughed softly. 'I think Jannet decides what's good for Jannet. It's a good thing too. Why should Nick object? From what she told me, he's extremely busy harvesting the vegetables. I imagine he'll be happy to know someone else is keeping her company part of the day. If you go, you may be stopping a family war!'

It was a tempting prospect. Sara liked

Jannet, though she didn't want to mull too much over what she thought about Nick. If he were busy in the fields all day, she wouldn't see much of him anyway. It wouldn't cost her much if she stayed with them, she could help when Jannet wanted her to, she could explore the locality, and, like Eddie mentioned, perhaps she would still have time to leave and go somewhere else.

She felt uplifted and cheerful. 'Tell her I'll come!'

10

Sara borrowed Eddie's GPS. It was her first long journey driving a car, and she was a little nervous, but soon began to enjoy the feeling of freedom. She had more than enough room for her luggage, and Eddie had given her some rose bushes for Jannet. They were still in their pots and standing behind the seats. Aunt Hilda said she didn't understand why Sara wanted to help a woman she hardly knew, but it didn't stop her going.

Once she'd crossed the Channel, she took her time. She didn't mind when other cars went whizzing past or overtook, as she wanted to be careful. Not only was she a novice driver, but she was now driving on the wrong side of the road!

After making one short stop to have Aunt Hilda's sandwiches and flask of tea an hour or so after leaving the ferry, she turned into the driveway of Château Renault in the early afternoon. She relished the view of the old façade again when it came into sight. It seemed so familiar. She parked her car neatly on the side, making a mental note to ask where she could park permanently. Probably where Nick did, alongside the outbuildings.

She got out, stretched and then relaxed. The door opened and Jannet stood there, looking slightly awkward on crutches and with one white leg in plaster. She was wearing a flowery summer skirt with a matching T-shirt.

Sara hurried towards her and Jannet beamed. 'Sara! Am I glad to see you! Thank you so much for sacrificing your plans to come here instead.'

'It isn't a sacrifice. How are you? Apart from feeling frustrated.'

'It is so irritating. You can't believe it! I can do anything with my hands just as before, but I'm limited in how I get anywhere. The crutches slow me down and Nick keeps checking up on me, which almost annoys me more!'

Sara laughed. 'How did it happen?'

'I tripped over a rake. Silly, I know. I left it lying on the ground and forgot all about it. At least I just tripped over the handle part and fell onto the stonework bordering the flowerbed. If I'd fallen in the other direction, I'd have fallen on the spiky part. Heaven knows what would have happened then. I've learned my lesson.'

'Was it a clean break?'

'Yes, in two places. Nick took me to the emergency room straight away, and they put me in plaster. Luckily he'd come down to fetch something to drink. That was nearly two weeks ago.'

'Very annoying I'm sure, but I'm here now to help you in any way I can.'

Jannet nodded. 'I want you to have a holiday, Sara, and I don't want to burden you with my work. I just thought if I could persuade you to come for a week or two, it would stop Nick fussing around me like a mother hen. When he knows someone else is in the house, he'll relax and concentrate on his own work. He's very busy harvesting at the moment. I'll go mad if he keeps rushing back and forth, especially as I know that he hasn't got the time to do it.' She turned awkwardly. 'Come through to the kitchen. I'll make you a cup of tea.'

Progress was slow. When they reached the large kitchen with its outsized solid wooden table and big dresser filled with blue china, Sara didn't try to interfere when Jannet started slowly gathering things to make tea.

'Sit down,' Jannet said. 'Did you have a good journey? How is Eddie?'

Sara did as requested. 'I had no trouble getting here, and Eddie is fine. He sent you a couple of roses. They're in their pots in the car. I left the window open so that they could get some fresh air.'

'That was kind of Eddie. I won't be able to plant them for a while, but if they're in pots that's OK. I have a spot in mind that will suit perfectly.'

'If you show me where, and give me instructions for exactly how, I'll plant them for you if you like. Here, let me pour the water into the teapot. If you drop a cup it won't matter, but if you drop a kettle of boiling water you'll be in a real pickle.'

Jannet laughed and nodded, then made way for Sara to finish the task. 'See, Sara? That's the difference between you and Nick. Nick just gets up and takes it all out of my hands. You explain why you think it would be better for you to do it.'

'I'm sure Nick doesn't mean any harm. He wants to help, but he's smothering you in the process.'

'Exactly! I know I need more time to do the simplest chores, and I'll have to neglect some of them for now, but I want to do as much as I can.'

As they sat at the table, Sara talked about the journey and how she'd enjoyed managing it on her own. Jannet chattered about the château and what was being harvested at the moment.

Sara took a sip of the tea. It tasted good. Cupping her hands around the mug, she asked, 'Why didn't you want Madeleine, or someone else from the village, to help?'

'Because I can tell you don't fuss! She does. I don't like it when someone treats me like a child.'

After a while, Sara got up and stacked their crockery in the sink. There was a pile of dirty dishes waiting there already. 'I'd like to do the washing up,' Jannet said, 'but it's difficult on crutches. I could sit down on a chair and have both hands free, but none of them are high enough.'

Sara remembered seeing an old high stool in one of the outbuildings. She left Jannet, hurried across to the barn with the machinery, and found what she was looking for. It was covered in dust, but she brushed it off carried it back to the kitchen.

Jannet's eyes twinkled. 'I'd forgotten

about that stool. I can see what you mean. It's just the right height. If I open the door under the sink, I can sit on the stool and put my plaster-cast leg in the cupboard.'

Sara grinned. 'That's what I thought. I remembered seeing it when I was here last. I'll clean it up, and clear the cupboard under the sink, and you'll be able to tackle the washing up. In the meantime, I'll unload my car.'

'I already feel that I did exactly the right thing in trying to get you to come here.' Jannet beamed at her. 'I hope that you won't be sorry. I don't intend to saddle you with work, Sara. Please, bring your things inside. Your room is upstairs to the left and it's the second door on the right. Sheets and towels are in the bathroom cupboard at the end of the corridor. You'll have to make up your own bed, but I know you don't mind doing that.'

Sara shook her head. She placed a teacloth in an accessible place near the draining board and left Jannet to attack the dishes.

An hour later, she'd unpacked her things and made her bed. She skipped down the stairs and went back to the kitchen. The clean dishes were stacked neatly on the draining board. Without further ado, Sara picked them up and carried them to their appropriate place on the dresser.

'Sara, I'm going to start the evening meal,' Jannet said. 'If you fetch the potatoes and the other things I need, you can dump them here on the draining board, and I'll wash and peel everything.'

'What are you planning to make?'

'Now what do you call it in Britain . . . ?' She tried to recall and was successful. 'A casserole, that's right. Layers of vegetables and meat.'

'That sounds good. What do you need, and where do I find it?' With Jannet's instructions, she soon found all the ingredients, and piled them on the side. Jannet did seem happier now she had found something 'useful' to do.

'Why don't you take a look around and see if anything's changed since you were last here?' Jannet invited her.

Sara smiled. 'I don't suppose it has. It is only been a matter of weeks. I'll get the rose bushes out of the car, though.'

'If you don't mind, put them at the bottom of the steps in the rose garden. They'll have time to get used to the position before I actually plant them. Good thing they're in pots! That means they don't need to be planted immediately. I'll hobble around there to take a look at them after I've finished preparing our meal, and I'll phone Eddie later to thank him.'

'If you're sure I can't help . . . ?' Jannet shook her head. 'Right. I'll see to the roses, then go for a stroll, and see you later.'

'Do that!'

The rose garden looked fantastic. The flowers, a carpet of mixed colours, were in full bloom. The perfume in the air was wonderful. After Sara gave

Eddie's roses some water, she left them at the bottom of the steps. She breathed in deeply and looked around in satisfaction, deciding to set off in the direction of the outbuildings and the fields beyond.

She was a little apprehensive about meeting Nick again, but hadn't reckoned with meeting him quite so soon. Walking round the corner of the barn, she nearly bumped into him. They looked at each other, and surprise was written all over his face too. Sara presumed she looked just as startled. She became increasingly uneasy under his scrutiny, as the unexpected surge of affection she felt when she looked at him almost frightened her. She'd never felt anything like it before. Awkwardly she cleared her throat and stuck her arms behind her skirt.

'Nick! It's nice to see you again. I didn't expect to come back so soon, but for some reason Jannet seems to think I can help her cope better with the situation. She's very frustrated by her lack of mobility.'

He stood with his hands in the pocket of his jeans. His hair was out of control and his working boots were covered in dust. 'I didn't expect to see you soon again either. Had a good journey?'

'Yes, thanks. I've unpacked, and Jannet sent me out on an exploratory walk.'

'She's getting more short-tempered with every passing day. She's never been dependent on anyone, and she doesn't like the fact that she sometimes needs help now.'

Sara hoped her smile was noncommittal enough. 'I can imagine what it's been like. I think she'll be a lot happier if she's left to do as much as she can on her own. I left her making the evening meal.'

His eyebrows lifted, and she noted his skin had a deeper tone. He'd been working outside a lot since she'd seen him last.

'How's she managing that on her

own?' he asked. 'The crutches hamper her when she moves, and usually that means it's also risky for her to carry things around.'

'I fetched her the high stool from the barn. I saw it there that day you showed me your machinery. She's sitting on that in front of the sink right now. She's washed the dishes, and asked me to give her the vegetables, meat and the chopping block. I think she's glad to be doing something useful again.'

'She could fall off that stool.'

Sara managed a cautious reply. 'Nick, she could fall off a chair in the living room.'

He pulled his hands out of his pockets and shifted. 'I'll just go and check what she's doing.'

Sara reached out automatically and put a hand on his arm. 'Don't, Nick. Let her be. She's in no danger, and she hates being wrapped up in cotton wool. I could've stayed and watched her peel the carrots, but I can tell that she wants to be on her own and do something halfway normal. She knows you're worried, and she thinks you're fussing too much. It makes things worse.'

They were inches apart, and she was suddenly anxious to escape his glance. Something flickered in the back of his eyes before he shrugged his shoulders and spread his hands out. She was almost glad the contact was broken.

'If you're sure?' he said.

'I'm sure. I'll go back in a little while. She's all right! Get back to your work and leave her to do hers.' He turned and was about to set off again when Sara called after him. 'Oh, Nick! I was just wondering if it'd be more comfortable for her to have a wheelchair. What do you think? You have plenty of space for her to move around the furniture in the rooms, and I'm sure it'd be easier for her than coping with crutches. It might take a little persuasion for her to accept the idea, but you can leave that up to me. If a free one isn't part of your health care, we could hire one on a weekly basis.'

Nick did a slow turnabout and a grin split his face. His teeth looked very white. 'You are quite something, Sara. I hadn't thought of that. It's a great idea. She'd be mobile and very safe in a wheelchair. I'll look into it when I go in, but go ahead and mention it to her.' He chuckled and set off for the fields again. His hand waved above his head.

11

It took some persuading, but Jannet finally agreed to try a wheelchair around the house. She still used the stool when busy at the sink, but the wheelchair was a total success. Sometimes the footrest got in the way, but it gave her a lot more freedom because she could carry things around on her lap when moving from one spot to another. The rooms and hallways had plenty of room for a wheelchair. When Sara compared it to her aunt's small cottage, she knew that living in a big château had its advantages, although the heating bills must be horrific.

Although there were only three of them in the house, Sara didn't see very much of Nick. She heard him carrying Jannet's wheelchair downstairs from her bedroom in the morning, and saw him waiting until she came down using her crutches and was safely seated, but generally he was up and away before Sara started her day. During their evening meal, Sara felt torn by conflicting emotions when she sat opposite him. Sometimes the attraction she felt made her thoughts unmanageable, and she told herself to stop it. It was very, very stupid to think about Nick in a romantic way. Such an attraction would lead nowhere. His gaze seemed to rest a mite too long on her face sometimes, but she told herself he was being an attentative host. Jannet kept the conversation flowing with questions about his harvesting problems, telling him what they'd been doing, and repeating the gossip a young cleaning woman from the village brought with her.

Jannet's help was a friendly, generously curved woman with dark hair and dark eyes. She was married with two children and had been coming two days a week to help Jannet with the general cleaning for a couple of years. The château was too large for a single person to manage. Even now, they were barely able to keep things under control. At present, Anne kept up the appearance of tidiness when she busied herself with the cleaner and by keeping the bathrooms spick and span.

It was the busiest time of the year for Nick, and he was usually tired when he came in from the fields. Sara could understand why he often carried his mother's wheelchair up to her room and left, after having his coffee and a looking at the news headlines.

Usually Sara and Jannet watched the TV or read. Jannet liked to play cards, and they sometimes played a couple of rounds of gin rummy; Jannet won nearly every time. Sara's time was free nearly all day and every day. She just made sure Jannet had everything that she needed, and did the shopping whenever it was necessary. Apart from that, Jannet told her that she should take off and explore the surrounding countryside, so she did.

It was fun to take off in her car with no set idea of where she was going and explore the local small villages and towns. She stopped for coffee or a snack whenever she felt like it. The weather was mostly fine, but there were occasional clouds hurrying across a grey sky, and showers. She drove to the coast a couple of times, and although she had her swimming togs with her, she decided it was too cold to actually take a dip. She admired the hardy figures who braved the elements and left their towels and rugs on the sandy beaches to frolic in the less-than-welcoming sea.

One afternoon she persuaded Jannet to make a visit to her rose garden. Sara took charge of the wheelchair, and then Jannet followed her down the steps using a crutch and the handrail for support. Jannet was delighted. She'd promised Sara not to go outside the house in the wheelchair on her own, as the gravel around the house would make things hard going without help.

Jannet was in her element among the sweet-smelling roses, with a basket on her lap and secateurs in her gloved hands. She deadheaded the roses as far as she could comfortably reach them from the path. Under Jannet's watchful eye, Sara moved between the remainder. She got scratched several times, but she didn't mind when she saw how much pleasure Jannet got from being there.

Sometimes Sara felt she was floating in a bubble of time. The days flowed into each other and she was wrapped in the cocoon of Brittany, Jannet and Nick. Now and then she felt she'd never lived anywhere else. It was like belonging to a real family.

Early one morning towards the end of Sara's first week at the château, Madeleine paid Jannet a visit. She explained she'd been staying with a relative in Paris and had only heard about Jannet's accident when she returned yesterday. She'd come straight over. Jannet kissed her on her cheeks and gestured to a nearby chair.

The two younger women exchanged greetings, but eyed each other cautiously. There was no reason Sara should feel be bothered, but the usual kind of small talk came out awkwardly and sounded forced. She guessed that Madeleine was annoyed that someone from England, whom Jannet barely knew, was assisting the older woman. Well if she liked Nick, surely she would have relished the chance to come over and help.

Sara decided to leave them and take off on her next outing. 'I'm going to Quimper this morning, Jannet. Do you need something?'

Jannet shook her head. 'No, thanks. You did the shopping yesterday. I have everything.' She looked out of the window. 'Take a jacket; it might rain.'

'I always have one in the car. I'll see you later. Bye, Madeleine!'

'Bye!'

Sara ran upstairs to get her bag, glad to escape. Madeleine didn't welcome her presence, but it wasn't hard to understand why. She'd grown up here, and knew Nick and Jannet very well. Sara wished she could be honest and tell Madeleine that there was no reason for her to feel ousted or green-eyed. In a couple of weeks she'd be gone again.

She spent a pleasant day, and even went as far as Carnac to see the famous menhirs and dolmen there. She took her time, and it was late afternoon when she got back. She went straight to the kitchen via the terrace, and her heart jolted and her pulse pounded when she found Nick already sitting at the table talking to Jannet. She told herself it was the sheer surprise of finding him there. It didn't mean more than that.

Nick was still in his working gear. He looked dusty and his hair was a mess. After days of driving various machines through the fields, his tan had deepened. His long legs were stuck out in a straight line that ended with his rugged working boots. He looked up and smiled, and the whiteness of his teeth stood out in his face.

Sara felt a surge of excitement and smiled back at him. 'What are you doing here? It's early for you. We don't usually see you until just before Jannet puts the food on the table.'

He ran his hand through his dark hair, but as it was tangled anyway, it didn't make much difference. 'We've finished the biggest order and got it all out on time. Some of the smaller customers are due in the next couple of days, but they're much easier to handle.' He got up. 'I'll get cleaned up and be back in time for dinner. I've got an appetite like a bear.'

'You look like one too,' Jannet said. She looked at the kitchen clock. 'Half an hour!'

Nick went, and Sara was almost glad of the respite. It gave her time to order her thoughts properly and prove to herself that she was immune to him. She told herself the reaction was only because she hadn't expected to see him and he was an attractive man. She turned her attention to Jannet and told her where she'd been. 'Can I help?'

'If you're going upstairs, you can take the water jug into the dining room on your way if you like. Nick can carry the rest of the meal in when he comes down.'

As always, the food was delicious. Sara decided she should look over Jannet's shoulder more often to see what she did. Nick's hair was still wet from the shower, and neatly combed. In a fresh shirt and clean jeans, he looked a different man, and his cologne drifted pleasantly across the table.

'Did you like Quimper and Carnac?' Jannet asked.

Nick looked up. 'That's quite a trip from here. You went via country roads?'

With her fork in mid-air, Sara said, 'Yes, but I enjoyed it. Country roads aren't so busy, and I have all the time in the world. If I'd felt nervous or frustrated, I would've turned back. I enjoyed both places, for different reasons of course.'

'You seem to like Brittany,' he said.

'I do. I like it very much. I can't explain why. Perhaps it's because people are so friendly, or because I like the untamed scenery.' She smiled at Jannet. 'Or perhaps it's because the food here is so wonderful.'

Nick nodded in approval. Jannet smiled and said, 'You make cooking a pleasure because you're prepared to try anything. Some strangers won't if they don't recognize what it is. For me, cooking is enjoyment most of the time. I do have days when I don't enjoy it much, but that's usually because I have too much to do elsewhere. You need time, fresh ingredients, and good recipes. Eventually you do without recipes and just cook. Do you cook at home?'

'Not much,' Sara replied. 'I don't get much of a chance. Aunt Hilda cooks simple but quite tasty meals. British cooking doesn't have the best reputation. I don't suppose I'll ever be a good cook like you.'

Jannet brushed her words aside. 'You can learn anything if you set your mind to it. I never did much cooking until I married, although I did grow up in a household where my mother and grandmother both enjoyed cooking, and that's a big advantage. Young wives today don't have the time their mothers and grandmothers had because they're working wives and mothers, but there's still a strong tradition of cooking in France. I hope it doesn't disappear completely.'

Addressing Sara, Nick said, 'There's a road race on Saturday, followed by a local dance. Would you like to go?'

It was unexpected, and she felt a warm glow somewhere inside. 'A cycle race?'

He nodded. 'Our equivalent of the Tour de France.' He smiled. 'Most of the participants are semi-professionals, but some locals have a go. People turn out to cheer them on, and then there's a dance with all the trimmings, where the winner is declared and presented with a cup.'

'Perhaps Jannet would like to go. I'm not much of a dancer.'

'I'll come as far as the main road to cheer the cyclists,' Jannet said, 'but for obvious reasons I'm not very interested in the dancing part of the evening. Do go, Sara! It's usually a lot of fun.'

Nick tilted his head to the side. 'I love my mother, but even I draw the line at partnering her to our Bal Populaire, even if she was able to stand on her own two feet, which she can't.'

'But perhaps you'd rather go with someone local,' Sara said. 'You don't need to feel you have to be polite just because I'm here.' She didn't want to mention Madeleine's name.

'I'm not just being polite,' he insisted. 'I'm asking you because I think you'd enjoy it.'

Taking a deep breath that she hoped wasn't too audible, she nodded. 'Then thanks, I'd like to come. Is it a dress-up thing?'

'No. The women seem to make more

of an effort than usual, but nothing too fancy.'

Jannet added, 'Anything goes these days — trousers, dresses, costumes. You can dress up or dress down, whatever you prefer.'

'Then I can't go wrong.'

Nick shook his head. 'I'll never understand why women make such a fuss about what they wear. It's like my vegetables in the end. It's not what's on the outside that counts, it's what's inside and how it tastes that matters!'

Nick and Sara washed up. He was clearly relaxed because the estate work was going well. He still had other customers to supply with various vegetables, but the order he'd finished today was a major one and had been his biggest headache. As they worked side by side, he talked about past dances and some of the antics people got up to. Sara also learned the evening was rounded off with a display of fireworks at midnight. She stacked everything where she thought it should be, and

Nick went off to take a last look round before he finished for the day.

After watching the news, they decided to play Monopoly because Nick said he wouldn't play cards, his reason being that his mother always won! They had an enjoyable time and the two women bankrupted him. In the end he owed them both so much money that he gave up. He opened a bottle of special wine and they watched a documentary about La Reunion. Sara was determined to concentrate on the television and she vowed she would not to look in his direction, although the temptation to do so was great. Uncontrolled thoughts galloped through her brain and her concentration often slipped. She was already looking forward to Saturday, more than when she'd had a date with someone else before, and she knew it was because it was Nick. She wondered briefly how Madeleine would feel. Well, she couldn't help it if the other woman wasn't his choice of companion for the evening. Perhaps he was just being polite to a foreign visitor. Sara decided not to worry about it. He'd asked her and she'd accepted.

12

On Saturday afternoon they went to the main road via the continuation of the pathway Sara had used to get from the village to Château Renault on that first day. They had a bit of a struggle to get the wheelchair through the gap in the hedge, but it was smooth going after that. When they reached the main road, some of Jannet's neighbours were already gathered there. There were groups of other spectators too, but Sara didn't recognize any of them, and she didn't see Madeleine either. The neighbours greeted them, fussed around Jannet, and were clearly keen to inspect the foreigner from England at close quarters. The weather was kind. There were grey clouds far above, but hardly any wind. No one knew exactly when the group of cyclists would go by, and people gossiped and passed the time by shouting to their neighbours and anyone else they thought worthy of their words of wisdom.

When the leading cyclist whizzed past, he was a couple of seconds ahead of the rest of the field. He was recognized and people weren't surprised to see he was in the lead. The spectators clapped hard, but they were waiting for local contenders who had no hope of winning. Whenever a familiar face passed them on his bike, the shouting grew louder, and the most popular words seemed to be *'Allez! Allez!'*

Sara wondered if the cyclists were mindful of the shouting and comments. The remarks thrown in their direction were probably more colourful than she assumed, but she didn't catch every word. Some of it was in the Breton language anyway. It was fun to just wait, and to listen to the raucous comments as each cyclist or batch of cyclists passed them. One group contained a familiar face. She looked up at

Nick. 'Heavens! There's André!'

He laughed. 'Yes, the idiot has taken part in the race as long as I can remember. He hasn't a snowball's hope in hell of winning unless all the others die on the way, but there's no stopping him. He says he'll keep trying until he's too old.'

'I think he's very plucky, especially if he knows he hasn't a chance of winning.'

'Do you?' He studied her speculatively. 'In favour of the underdog, eh?'

'Probably. It's nice to see a familiar face. Did you ever take part?'

He laughed. 'Only once, years ago. André persuaded me. We trained for weeks beforehand, but it didn't do much good. I thought my lungs would burst by the time I actually finished the course, and I was one of the last to arrive.'

'But if you stuck it out to the end, that's what it's all about.'

Gradually the participants dropped to single individuals who had to stand

156

on their pedals to conquer the slight incline ahead of them. They received the same encouragement as the leading cyclist. Feeling slightly disappointed, Sara looked down the empty road. 'That was it?'

'Uh, uh! They'll be back on the second circuit soon. They go round three times.'

Jannet produced some red wine and plastic cups from the bag on the wheelchair. They stood enjoying the cheerful company and waiting for the reappearance of the leading cyclist again. Sara noticed that other groups were also toasting and raising their glasses. Laughter and camaraderie were in the air as the afternoon wore on. Sara was almost sorry when the cyclists passed for the last time. From their diminishing numbers, even she could guess that a lot of the original starters wouldn't make it to the end. Nick and Jannet shouted their goodbyes to neighbours and friends and Nick pushed the wheelchair home.

The track was narrow and brambles and bushes framed the path, but most of the time Sara was able to walk alongside Nick. 'What about the presentation?' she asked. 'You said the winner gets a cup.'

'That will be part of the evening entertainment.'

The branches were intertwined above their heads and formed a tunnel of green. Birds sang in the undergrowth. Sara never ceased to appreciate nature at its best in this place. It had been an enjoyable afternoon and she'd spent it with nice people.

Jannet had announced again that she wouldn't change her mind and go to the evening events in the village. 'There's a good programme on TV. I can't wander around and talk to people like I usually do, so there's no point in going. It's a pity, because it's one of the few times in the year I have a chance to enjoy a twirl, but there will be other years.'

Sara was glad there was a pause

between the afternoon's events and setting off to the Bal Populaire. She had time to have a shower and change into her prettiest floral summer dress. It was sleeveless with a V-neck, flared skirt, and matching bolero. Her sandals were flat and comfortable. She took longer than usual with her make-up, and the final result was pleasing and she felt good. Nick was in the hallway when she came down the wide staircase. He looked at her and gave a low whistle. 'You look great!'

Colour flooded her cheeks. He wore classical trousers with a red polo shirt and comfortable loafers. She could tell he'd showered because his hair looked tamed, though it was also damp. A faint smell of his aftershave drifted towards her. It was a familiar aroma to her these days; a mixture of sandalwood with lemon or something similar.

'Thank you, kind sir!' she said. 'I must say you look good too. We've both made an effort, haven't we?'

He grinned and his eyes sparkled in

the shadows as she neared him. 'Let's see if my mother needs anything before we take off. Do you want to drive there, or shall we walk?'

Sara thought quickly. Walking would give them more time to be on their own. They were often together, but seldom alone. She didn't understand why it was important, but the thought popped into her mind when he'd given her a choice, and it felt right to answer. 'Let's walk,' she said. He nodded.

Nick carried his mother's wheelchair upstairs. Jannet was sitting comfortably in front of the TV, and she promised to take her time with her crutches when she climbed the stairs to go to bed. She laughed. 'Don't worry about me. Have a good time, you two. I'll be careful, promise. Oh, before I forget — Eddie phoned just now. He's organized the furniture removals, and the company will bring everything over one day next week.'

Nick nodded. 'We'll have to store it in one of the barns until you decide where you want to put it. If the removal firm don't send enough people to help with the unloading, I'll get Yvré or one of the others down from the top field to help us.'

Jannet nodded. 'When we were talking, I persuaded Eddie to come over and spend a few days with us. I'd like to see him again.'

'Good idea! He's a nice chap, and good company. Perhaps Sara can sort out one of the bedrooms for him? It would save you the hassle.' Sara nodded, and he announced, 'We're off!'

Jannet nodded. 'Enjoy yourselves, and dance one extra one for me. Greetings to anyone who asks after me.'

Nick nodded and reached out for Sara's hand. She felt a lurch of excitement. He only loosened his hold when they reached the gap in the hedge.

They followed the path until they were alongside the field where Sara had first set eyes on him. It was pitch dark, and the moon above them was a bright silver disc. It was their only source of light, and silence reigned all round. When Sara glanced over the top of the dark outlines of the hedges at the fields and their surroundings beyond, it gave her a strange feeling. Nick knew the way like the back of his hand, though, and when she almost stumbled, he took her hand again and held it firmly.

'I walked along this path to school every day and all through my teenage years,' he said. 'The path and I are good friends.'

They walked in silence, and his hand felt cool and smooth as he clutched hers tightly. Even though he worked hard on the estate, working gloves seemed to keep any callousing and roughness at bay. Sara had never felt so alive. Nick had a presence that fascinated her. Looking back, it began from the moment she first saw him. He was virile with a firmness and strength she admired, and had a polished yet casual style. She'd met other good-looking, interesting men, but not one of them had fascinated her the way Nick did. She couldn't explain why. It had nothing to do with the estate, or with the situation. It must be the man himself.

His voice broke the silence. 'You all right? It's not far now. We've almost reached the church.'

She cleared her throat. 'Fine, thanks. I can't pretend I've walked past many lonely churchyards in the dark, but as long as you're with me I'm OK.' He laughed softly in the darkness and increased the pressure of his figures to reassure her for a moment. Her heartbeat sped up as she enjoyed the delicious sensation.

'Don't tell me you're afraid of ghosts?' he whispered teasingly.

'I've never met one, but who can tell? There are probably as many lost souls buried in this churchyard as anywhere else. Apparently troubled souls can stay in a kind of limbo until some brave person sorts out the complications that tie them to this world. Once that's done, they can take off for the next level, whatever that means.'

With dry amusement in his voice, Nick said, 'I don't believe in ghosts. I've passed this place hundreds and hundreds of time in the dark and never seen a single floating spectre.'

He paused and brought them to a halt. Sara faced him and managed to pick out the main features of his face. He went on, 'I do recall one strange experience, though. André and I had been to the bistro in the village. He'd left his bike at our place and had to come back with me. He decided we had to take a shortcut from the village across the fields to get to this path. You can imagine, even though you don't know him very well yet, that once he makes up his mind he can't be deterred. Anyway, we got as far as the church, and I made my way round the graves to get to the gateway on this side. When I looked back, André had disappeared. I wondered what the hell had happened to him. After a few minutes of silence, rising panic, and recalling all the stories about spirits and ghouls and manifestations, I decided something was really wrong. I couldn't see a thing in the dark, so I decided I'd have to go back to the village for the priest and get some help to search the graveyard. I was about to leave when his head popped out above the edge of a freshly dug grave.'

Sara couldn't control her loud burst of laughter. 'No! Really?'

'I could have killed him. He put the fear of God into me, and he made things worse because he thought it was a great joke and was laughing like an idiot.'

'I can imagine. It was obviously fun for him, but I'm sure I would've panicked straight away and screamed at the top of my voice.'

'Believe me, the effect of a white face popping up from an empty grave in the middle of the night is scary, very scary. Even though I don't believe in ghosts.'

'It would scare most people to death.

André's quite a character, isn't he?'

'We've been friends since kindergarten. He's always been slightly mad, but he's often spot-on with his ideas. I always thought it was a pity he didn't go to university, but he didn't want to. He's impulsive and funny, and also loyal and dependable. He's the friend I turn to in an emergency. I can always count on him.'

'That says everything about someone,' Sara mused. 'I think real friends are almost a kind of self-completion, aren't they? You're steady and serious; André is a bit crazy. The opposites work together to make a whole. My friend Kelly is outgoing, flamboyant, and extravagant, while I'm quieter and more restrained. We knock the jagged edges off each other and still stay friends.'

Nick's aftershave drifted across the night air. 'I've never thought of it in that way, but you may be right. I bet André's mother gave him hell when he turned up with his clothes covered in mud from the graveyard!'

They carried on, and Sara had the desire to just go on walking with Nick forever. The dance in the village couldn't be better than drifting along a dark and empty country lane with this man. As they drew closer, they could see a glow above the trees; and then when they were closer still, the sound of boisterous music shattered the silence. Entering the small village square, Sara was surprised how delightful it looked, like something out of a fairy tale, with strings of coloured lights uniting the trees along the edges. The four sides of the square were jam-packed with people between stands that were wafting out appetizing aromas. Once she'd adjusted to the light, Sara took in all the details. Music from a live band was blaring away, and there was already a crowd of people twirling around in the centre. The tune sounded like a kind of polka.

They passed the main stand, where trophies were on display and microphones waited for the organizers to announce the winners and present them with their prizes. Here and there children ran back and forth in the crowd. Sara wondered how long their parents would allow them to stay. People shouted at Nick and he responded. Sara noticed their inquiring looks, but Nick gave them no chance to question him or stop them. He held her hand and pulled her along with him so as not to lose contact in the crowd. They ended up in a far corner, where he spotted André with some others.

Fun was in the air, and Sara was prepared to enjoy herself, especially knowing she was Nick's official partner for the evening.

13

The group of young people they joined were friendly. André grabbed Sara straight away and kissed her cheeks.

She smiled. 'Well done, André! You finished the course?'

'Naturally! Not my best result, but I did finish.'

Nick introduced the others, and Sara tried to remember the names. The men viewed her with interest, the women with curiosity. Madeleine stood in the middle of them all. She held out her cheek for Nick's kiss and acknowledged Sara with a nod. She was trying to appear friendly, but Sara could see in her eyes that she didn't welcome Sara's inclusion in the evening's fun.

Sara tried to sympathize. If Madeleine was in love with Nick, and had been hoping for years that they would become more than just childhood friends, the

169

appearance of a strange woman on his arm, even if she was just a visitor, must be disheartening. But Sara didn't control Nick's motives for doing anything, and neither did Madeleine. She wished she could reassure her that she was just passing through and this evening wouldn't change what the future would bring. She tried to relax.

Nick went off to get them something to drink while Sara listened to André describe his part in the race. Her French had been quite good before she'd arrived, but by now she had next to no difficulty keeping up with the conversation or expressing herself.

Luckily, or intentionally, the village square was tarmacked in the centre, although the side pavements were often cobblestoned. There was an ancient oak dead centre that was decorated with multiple garlands of coloured lights. Together with all the other lights hung between trees and other supports along the periphery, the whole square looked very festive and colourful. More and more people joined the throng, and the area in the middle was soon full of happy couples dancing to the loud beat of the band coming from the main podium.

Nick returned and handed Sara a plastic tumbler. 'I thought you might like some cider.'

'Lovely, thanks.' She took a sip and appreciated the cool smoothness of the local brew.

Others joined them and the circle grew larger. Sara gathered that they were nearly all friends from schooldays. In the countryside, where people often lived apart, the children had stronger ties to old school friends. In towns, people came and went more often, which tended to make them less involved. The larger group broke up into smaller ones, and people wandered between them now and then. They all knew how to enjoy themselves. They laughed a lot, ate enthusiastically, and talked non-stop until it grew dark and insects arrived to annoy everyone.

Children scampered between people's feet, and Sara wondered why their parents weren't worried about where they were. At first she was nervous, but she soon felt better because everyone included her naturally in their conversation when they could.

Most of the men had to be persuaded to dance, whereas the women were impatient to be part of the whirling masses. André grabbed Sara and gave Nick her empty tumbler as he led her towards the dancing. Sara liked him because he was so effervescent and it was easy to laugh at his witticisms. No one seemed to have much skill on the dance floor, and she found herself trying out a kind of polka. After dancing for several minutes, the constant twirling and spinning around the available space made her dizzy. She was glad when the band broke off for a minute or two.

Nick must have been waiting for his chance, because he joined them and silently indicated with his thumb that his friend was relieved of his duties. He slid one large hand around Sara's waist and took possession of her other one in a firm grip. She had to look up at him. His mouth curled as if it were on the edge of laughter. Her breath hadn't yet steadied from the dancing, and when his body was so close to hers, it only intensified her emotions. She felt she knew him quite well by now, and she realized she was in danger of liking him too much. His eyes held her gaze, and she was afraid of losing herself in their depths and looking ridiculous. His firm features and the confident set of his shoulders were very familiar, and it would be easy to throw caution to the wind.

There was a moment or two of silence as they stood and watched each other. Then the band started up again, and Sara was pleased to hear softer and slower tones. Nick pulled her closer and she leaned against the hardness of his chest. His chin rested on her head, and she decided to give common sense a day off. She loved being with him. She'd developed a lot of respect for him as well, particularly how he'd coped with unexpected problems in his life. Dreamily, she wished she could stay with him forever. Then she suddenly realized with clarity that she was falling in love with Dominique Rogard.

Thereafter, Sara didn't register if the dance was long or short. Her thoughts were in chaos the whole time, even though she enjoyed every second of being in Nick's arms. It was foolish to fall in love with him, she told herself. They were planets apart in many ways.

When the music ended, somehow she managed to face him and then withdraw from his arms. With one arm still around her waist, he guided her back to the others. She was glad no one knew her well enough to notice that she was much too busy with her own thoughts to concentrate on what was said. There was a lot of chatter and laughter as the evening progressed.

When Nick went off to get them something new to drink, Sara went to the portable toilets parked in a row on the other side of the square.

She didn't need to go to the toilet, but she needed a few moments alone. She stood looking into the darkness under the branches of the bordering trees, took a deep breath, and told herself she'd manage somehow. She just had to adjust and hide her feelings from the others.

A familiar voice broke into her thoughts. Madeleine and another woman were outside the cabins, waiting. Madeleine's voice drifted across to Sara, and it didn't sound friendly.

'Who does she think she is, coming here and acting as if she belongs? She doesn't know one end of a tractor from the other. What does she know about farm work, or about how Nick has struggled to survive? I don't understand why Jannet has to have her here.'

'She doesn't have to know which end of a tractor is which,' Madeleine's companion answered. 'It's only important that she doesn't look like the back end of a tractor. Looks are the first thing men notice, and she *is* pretty. You must admit that.'

'If you like that sort of prettiness.'

'I don't think you should antagonize her. Nick would notice and he might not like it. Remember how he stuck up for Anne even though she deserved to be ignored when she dropped Paul?'

Madeleine's voice was sulky. 'I'm trying very hard to conduct myself with decorum. But when you've known Nick as long as we all have, and you see a stranger walk into our midst and turn things upside down, it's not fair.'

'But it isn't just Nick who likes her, is it? André already likes her too. To be honest, I'm sure we can all like her if we make an effort. There's no talk of her staying permanently, so there's no point in you worrying, is there?'

Sounding grouchy, Madeleine grunted something that could have been agreement.

'Oh look, there's one free,' her companion said. 'Are you desperate, or can I go first?'

'Go ahead!'

A few seconds later, another cabin further down the line was free and Madeleine disappeared inside. Sara left her hiding-place quickly and set off to join the others again.

It was clear that Madeleine was jealous, but Sara couldn't help that. If they knew each other better, Sara could have cleared the air. Nick was bound hand and heart to his estate, and she herself was rooted in England.

Sara tried to enjoy what was left of the evening. His friends seemed to accept her without much trouble (even though Madeleine clearly didn't). They wandered along the stands and had something to eat here and there, then watched the presentation of the cup to the winner of the cycle race amid much clapping and cheering. Close to midnight there was a small fireworks display. Sara had seen more elaborate spectacles, but all that mattered was that she was with Nick, and all day had been lovely and something to remember. Who cared if there weren't that many colourful rockets and bangers?

The music and the dancing continued. Sara danced with some of the others and with Nick again. Her cheeks were bright red by the time people started to talk about calling it a day. Nick eyed her and lifted his brows.

'What do you say? Had enough?'

She nodded. 'I've really enjoyed it, and all of your friends are nice. I didn't feel like a stranger, but if you want to stay just say so.'

'Good.' He held out his arm. 'Let's go then, without making a lot of farewells. Some have left already, and others are about to leave too.'

Sara tucked her arm through his and they set out for the path from the corner of the square. She almost asked who was taking Madeleine home, but realized it might seem strange if she did.

After all the activities and noise, a

couple of yards along the path they were surrounded by silence once more, and Sara enjoyed the feeling of Nick and herself alone in the world. He didn't seem to mind her arm through his, so she made no attempt to free herself. She just relished the moment silently. The stillness of the night was a balm for the soul. Sara didn't need to feel uncertain or frightened as long as she was with Nick.

'Thank you for taking me, Nick,' she said. 'I like your friends, and I like your village. The cycle race and the Bal Populaire were great.'

He reached out in the darkness and squeezed her hand resting on his arm. 'I'm glad. I was afraid you might find it dull.'

'Did you? Why?'

The profile of his dark shoulders lifted and fell in the darkness. 'I don't know. I suppose I assumed that you usually go to more sophisticated gatherings — town discos, proper dances, that sort of thing.'

'I don't like discos, and there aren't many proper dances these days. Even if there were, they wouldn't be much use to me. I can't dance.'

He laughed softly. 'You managed to circle around back there.'

'Anyone can manage a polka if they count one, two, three and shuffle their feet in time. I was worried about having enough stamina to finish sometimes, but I enjoyed myself, and that's the truth.'

Nick came to a halt suddenly and disengaged their arms. Then he reached forward and his large hands rested her shoulders. Sara couldn't see his face clearly in the dark, but his eyes mirrored what light there was as he looked down at her. There was a tingling in the pit of her stomach. His head slowly descended, and she felt the sweet sensation of his lips on hers. There was a dreamy intimacy to the kiss, and her emotions whirled and skidded. She was powerless to resist, and she didn't want to.

Sara didn't want to analyse why Nick had kissed her or what it meant. Happiness filled her as her heart jolted and her pulse pounded away. She delighted when he released her lips only to kiss her again a moment later. Finally he brushed a gentle kiss across her forehead, and without a word he slipped his arm around her shoulder, turned her towards the pathway again, and guided them on their way. With her heart still thumping erratically, a delightful feeling of excitement filled her. She savoured his closeness and didn't intend to spoil the moment by asking him questions. Perhaps he'd say something she didn't want to hear. She wanted to enjoy the moment and store the memory for a time when tonight was just a dream from the past.

Nick seemed to be lost in his own thoughts, and they went on for a few minutes longer. Glancing briefly at the big silver globe above them in a black velvet heaven, Sara could only imagine what it would be like to belong to Nick body and soul; not just for this evening, but forever.

They neared the church and Sara decided to break the silence. 'I wanted to ask André if the ghosts were after him to get their own back since that night, but I forgot.'

Nick chuckled. 'I expect the ghosts realize it would be a waste of time. André wouldn't take any notice.' He paused. 'He and I are going sailing next weekend if the weather holds. Would you like to come?'

With her heart still beating wildly, she managed to sound quite natural. 'I told you that I can't sail, didn't I? I'd only get in the way.'

He said softly, 'No you won't. You can just sit and let us do the work.'

'Nick, you don't have to entertain me. You work very hard on the estate, and you deserve to spend your leisure time enjoying yourself without someone like me to hold you back.'

Laughter floated up from his throat and he squeezed her shoulder. 'Sara, you wouldn't be holding me back. I wouldn't ask you if I didn't want you along. You know me well enough by now to know when I'm lying!'

She threw caution to the wind. 'Then in that case, I'd love to, as long as there's a life jacket!'

His chuckle echoed through the darkness as they progressed down the final bit of the path. Reaching the gap in the hedge, Nick held it aside, and she slipped through before he followed. The main door was still open. Sara wondered if it was ever locked. The house was silent expect for the ticking of a grandfather clock in the corner of the hall. They both looked through the open door into the sitting room, but it was dark and there was no sign of Jannet. She seemed to have managed the trip to her bedroom without mishap.

They crossed the hallway together and went up the stairs side by side. Sara's room was further down the corridor. She whispered, 'Goodnight, and thanks again.' She could see his face more clearly here in the house, and she detected a flicker in his intense eyes.

His large hands cradled her face, and his kiss this time was surprisingly gentle. 'Sleep well, Sara!'

She nodded in the darkness without knowing if he could see her. Totally confused by what had happened that evening, she left him standing and walked on without looking back. As she went, she told herself that Nick was just showing interest in her because she happened to be around and he quite liked her. He knew there was no future in it for both of them. One day he'd end up married to Madeleine, or someone like her. Sara didn't want to think about that; it hurt too much. She loved him, she admitted to herself, but it was silly to imagine that Nick wanted anything more than an innocent flirt with a visitor from England. He needed a partner who could drive a tractor and harvest the crops; someone who knew all about the land and could help him run the estate. Sara wasn't even French! She hadn't resisted his kisses because she longed for them, and the temptation was too great, but she had to be more careful in future. The deeper she fell in love, the harder it would be to leave him. She had known Nick was someone special from the very beginning, but it didn't mean there would be a happy end.

Her last waking thought before she finally drifted into sleep was that however much she loved Nick, and always would, he wasn't for her. She had to face reality.

14

The next day Sara wondered if anything would seem different when they next met. Nick was already out before she came down for breakfast, so she had to wait until late afternoon for his reappearance. Jannet asked how Sara had enjoyed herself the night before, and she could reply in all honesty that it was one of the best evenings she'd ever had. Jannet nodded and went on to chat about past Bal Populaires. Then Sara went to the local supermarket for Jannet, which was followed by a few hours on the terrace with a good book, even though she was finding it difficult to concentrate. She kept reading the same thing twice while dreaming of other things.

When Nick came into the kitchen later that afternoon, he looked at Sara longer than usual, but she couldn't decide whether or not it meant that their relationship had changed. Feeling nervous, she turned away and busied herself by laying the table for their evening meal. From where she was in the dining room, she heard Nick briefly exchanging news with his mother before he took the stairs two at a time to freshen up for the meal.

Jannet's presence helped to restore normality during the meal. Nick's and Sara's eyes met as he went over the festivities of the previous evening for his mother, and Sara nodded and managed a smile and told herself not to start reading too much meaning into Nick's kisses. Nowadays, a kiss could signify anything from casual friendship to romantic passion. She wasn't brave enough to try to find out what he'd been thinking. She didn't want to be hurt.

When Sara heard that Jannet had some office work for the estate that she needed Nick's help with, she volunteered to clear the kitchen. She was glad to busy her hands and not have to sit, knowing Nick was so close and yet so far away. By the time she finished and had made herself comfortable, she heard the front door closing. Jannet came in and said that Nick had just had a phone call from a friend. Their tractor had broken down and they'd asked if he could help, so he'd set out straight away.

Sara nodded, almost glad she could relax. The uncomfortable and uptight feeling she had at the moment when she was with Nick was foreign to her. Usually she had no problem confronting someone with an honest question, even if the answer didn't please her. She preferred to know exactly where she stood, and had never had difficulty talking about her own point of view — but she was not brave enough to talk things through with Nick. What could she say? 'Hey, Nick what did that mean last night when you kissed me? Was is just for fun, or did it signify more than that?' She'd be embarrassed before the words left her mouth, because perhaps it had meant nothing at all to him, and would only show him that she was too eager and naive.

She didn't see him again that evening. The next morning, Jannet told her that Eddie had phoned to say the furniture would be on its way that afternoon, and he would follow in his own car. They should arrive sometime the next day. Sara spent most of the morning getting one of the bedrooms ready, as it needed some fresh paint and new wallpaper. The carpet was rather threadbare as well, but the sparse furniture was good. Like most rooms in an old building, it had a special charm. The view from the window across the garden and towards the distant fields was lovely. The room hadn't been used for a while, and as the help from the village wasn't due today and Jannet wanted Eddie to feel comfortable, Sara had been asked if she'd get it ready. She was glad to have something to do, though while she was busy her thoughts still circled round Nick. Eventually she came to the conclusion that she had to act as if nothing had happened between them. She didn't want to embarrass him or herself.

After polishing the furniture, cleaning the carpet and the surrounds with a vacuum, making up the bed with some fresh linen, and opening the windows to let in the fresh air, the room was ready. The bathroom was nearby, and Sara cleaned that too. By the time Nick came in from the fields that afternoon, she felt stronger.

Dark clouds had raced across the landscape, and Nick had got wet in the ensuing downpour. He left his boots by the doorway, and after a brief hello, sprinted past his mother and Sara in the kitchen to shower and change.

Jannet had been busy most of the morning making preparations for entertaining Eddie. Some cakes were ready in plastic containers, their lids still open as Jannet waited for them to cool down. She'd fried slices of paprika and aubergine, which were now marinating in oil and herbs together with juicy olives. Jannet had also made a pâté of minced meat, liver and onions, and she'd telephoned a local farmer for a chicken for the following evening's meal. When it arrived, it was yellow in colour, and Sara's surprised look led Jannet to explain that the chickens were fed with lots of corn and ran free in a large fenced-in area near the farmer's house. Sara had no doubt that it would taste wonderful.

That evening, Sara found that she could meet Nick's glance with equanimity even though her heartbeat quickened every time their eyes met. He seemed to watch her more closely too, but she tried not to interpret that in the wrong way. He had arranged to meet André and his other sailing partner and asked her if she'd like to come along. He seemed a little surprised when she shook her head.

'Thanks, Nick, but you don't need me in tow all the time. I must write to

Aunt Hilda, and I planned to do that this evening.'

He didn't protest, but he looked puzzled. He left soon after they finished the meal. Sara didn't notice how he looked back at her for a moment as he stood at the door. She and Jannet were on their way to the kitchen with the dishes. Jannet caught his expression, and she smiled quietly to herself before she went to the sink and began washing the dishes.

Sara presumed Madeleine would be one of the other friends Nick was meeting. A group of them often met up whenever they had time. The thought of him with other women burned inside, but it was perfectly natural, and it was a good thing for him, Sara told herself. Perhaps he and Madeleine would be a pair one day, working the estate side by side and having the kind of life Sara wished could be hers.

Jannet was more energized than usual next morning. She hurried everyone through their breakfast on the terrace, even though it was a beautiful, clear, cool morning. She wanted to complete her preparations.

Sara tidied the downstairs rooms and went upstairs to make the beds. She never went into Nick's room. It seemed right to help Jannet, because remaking a bed from a wheelchair was an awkward, time-consuming process; but Nick's room was Nick's business.

Later she drove to town to buy some cheese from the market. Jannet gave her a written list and Sara enjoyed wandering the stalls searching for the various items. When she got back, there was a large arrival van parked next to the outbuildings. Men were busy transporting the furniture inside. She saw Eddie standing next to Jannet, watching the men carry various bits of furniture into the barn. Sara could only guess what was inside, but she was sure Eddie knew, and that he'd marked and listed everything in a way that would make it easy to find later. They looked up and smiled as she came across and joined them. Eddie gave her a resounding kiss on her cheek, and somehow it was a great feeling to have someone she knew at hand again.

'Hello, Eddie! Had a good trip?'

'Splendid, my dear! I arrived before the removal van, but then they haven't been to this part of the world before, so they were at a disadvantage. Kelly sends her love. I met her yesterday in the supermarket.'

Sara felt guilty that she hadn't given much thought to her friend since she'd arrived in Brittany. 'Thanks. Did she say anything about that young manager from the building company who came to our protest meeting?'

'Apparently they're going out together. She spent most of the conversation talking about him and his job. It looks like she's met someone special at last. Don't know much about him, but he seems OK. Flashy car, plenty of money; that should suit Kelly down to the ground.' He looked down at Jannet. 'I was very surprised to find Jannet in a wheelchair, it gave me a bit of a shock. But then she explained it was your idea, to give her more mobility.'

Jannet laughed softly. 'It was a wonderful idea. It's made the world of difference. You know how independent I am. Trying to cope with crutches and do something at the same time was hell. Now I can manage most things, providing whatever I need is within reach.' She looked towards the barn. The men were still busy. 'Should I phone Nick and ask him to come and bring some of the men to help?'

Eddie shook his head. 'They know what they're doing. The weather is fine and they don't need to panic. I think they're booked on a ferry early tomorrow morning, so they have plenty of time. They loaded it all into the van, and I'm sure they want to get it out on their own too. Then if anything is broken, there won't be any argument about who's responsible.'

'Well I bet they'd welcome something

to eat and drink. Let's make them some sandwiches and coffee, Sara!'

They left Eddie still supervising things, and shortly afterward Sara returned with a tray of sandwiches and a couple of vacuum flasks of coffee. The men were glad to have a break, and Eddie was too. He came across to the two women, who were sitting outside the kitchen on the terrace. He made himself comfortable, accepted a cup of steaming coffee, and chatted to Sara about village news.

'What about the protest group?' she asked. 'Have they been busy?'

Eddie managed to look a little sheepish. 'I admit that some of the interest is dying, partly because we don't know yet if we definitely have something to protest about and partly because I've been busy with other things recently. I know that if someone doesn't keep reminding them, there's always a danger that they'll forget what it was all about.' He looked across meaningfully at Jannet, who laughed.

'Be honest!' she said. 'I expect some of the group wonder if you've gone over to the enemy.'

'Probably! Kelly is pally with the enemy too. But I hope we'll find a decent solution to all of this. I think that by now that people appreciate that it's silly to hope you'll keep Maldon House, but they also hope that whoever buys it will keep the balance between appearance and usefulness. If not, I'm afraid that you and I will end up in opposing camps, Jannet.'

She touched his hand briefly. 'I hope that will never happen, Eddie. You know that, don't you? The last I heard from the solicitors was that a wellness company was considering turning it into a hotel, but things were still in the initial stages and everything was up in the air.'

'Hmm! That wouldn't be bad for the village. The sort of people who want to go to those places aren't interested in making a commotion. In fact, they usually don't even leave the place or the grounds during their stay.'

'I thought that too, and it might even generate a couple of jobs — cleaning staff, kitchen staff, gardeners, reception, or repair companies. I don't know how serious they are, and the solicitor will be holding out for the best price possible. As soon as I know anything definite, I'll let you know, Eddie.'

He nodded. 'Oh, before I forget,' he said, turning to Sara. He reached into his inside pocket. 'Your aunt gave me these two letters for you. She didn't know how important they were.'

Sara hardly ever received any letters. She noticed that one was from an ex-boyfriend who'd moved to Exeter, but that would keep. She was curious about the other, and tried in vain to decipher the postmark. It looked official because the address was typewritten. Jannet and Eddie continued to chat about Maldon House as she opened the envelope and read.

Eddie looked across. 'Anything important, Sara? You look a bit taken aback.'

'I am. It's a letter from someone in Wales. I didn't know I had any relatives apart from Aunt Hilda. Apparently this woman is a cousin of my dad's. When she married, she moved to Scotland and later to Norway. Dad gave her some paintings of local beauty spots as a wedding present. She didn't know he'd died until there was a family get-together recently and people started talking about the past. Dad's sister was alive when he died, and she offered to take me, but Aunt Hilda insisted that because my mother was her sister, and she was the last of my parents to die, that meant she had more right. Aunt Hilda made no effort to keep in touch with my father's relatives, although it says here that my other aunt sent cards and letters for a couple of years. They were never answered, so in the end she gave up.'

Eddie looked startled. 'She kept the information about your other relatives hidden from you?'

'It looks like it. My Welsh aunt died a

couple of years ago, and it was only at this family get-together that my dad's cousin heard about what had happened and tried to find out where I was. I don't know how she did it, but she did. She thinks I should have the pictures and wants us to meet. She's invited me to visit her where she lives, on the Gower coast.' Sara's eyes misted over as she thought about lost opportunities. She'd always wished she had other relatives apart from Aunt Hilda.

Eddie blustered, 'That damned woman! I always thought she was cracked. Why would anyone stop an orphaned child from knowing she has other relatives?'

Sara paused before saying, 'I'm so glad this cousin has made the effort. I might have gone through the whole of my life thinking I had no one else.'

Jannet viewed her sympathetically. 'And from the contents of the letter, it looks like you have other relatives too.'

Sara nodded and managed a shaky smile. Brushing the beginnings of a tear or two from her cheek, she said, 'I'll go and see her of course.'

'Here, drink some coffee,' Jannet said. 'Yes, you must, as soon as you can. Just think — you now have a family, even if it is a distant one.'

Sara took a sip and steadied her thoughts. 'Yes. I'm really glad. It's like winning the lottery!'

Eddie laughed. 'I'm delighted for you, Sara. This woman sounds like a nice person. She went to the trouble of finding out where you were as soon as she found out about your existence. Wait until I see your aunt!'

Sara knew there was no point in trying to stop him reproaching Aunt Hilda. As the reality of what was in the letter sank in, she was glad when Eddie declared he was off to check progress with the removers, and Jannet announced she had to see to things in the kitchen. It left Sara free, and she decided a solitary walk would be a perfect way of absorbing the news. She waved to Eddie talking to the removal men in the yard and went towards the hedge.

She walked up the incline until she reached the field where she'd seen Nick on his tractor that first day. Today the field was empty and the ground had been turned ready for the next planting. The sun shone down nicely and a warm summer breeze lifted her hair.

She found a gap and strolled across the field. Leafy trees lined the boundary on that side, the beginnings of a small wood. Sara found a mossy spot among the visible roots of one of the trees overlooking the field, then sat down and thought about her long-lost relations. She couldn't help thinking about Nick too, and she even briefly wished she'd fallen in love with someone else at home in England. It would have been more logical and more sensible, but love didn't function like that.

She was still in deep thought when minutes later her attention was caught by someone coming across the field.

15

Her heartbeat increased measurably when she saw Nick. He was wearing a blue workshirt that strained across his broad shoulders, and jeans that hugged his slim hips. He waved when he saw she'd noticed him. Minutes later, he threw himself down next to her.

She tried to sound flippant. 'What are you doing here? Skiving as usual?'

He gave her a smile that resulted in her innards having collywobbles. 'No. I came down to see if help was needed with the furniture, but Eddie has everything under control.' He bent one knee, and his other leg was stuck out in front of him in a straight line. He reached forward for a blade of grass and played with it. 'Eddie told me about your letter; about you finding out you have other relatives. That must've been a shock. How do you feel?'

'I'm fine. It's good news. I was startled at first, but it's very comforting to know I have a distant family, even if I don't know any of them.'

He nodded. 'I bet!'

'How did you know I was here?'

'Eddie saw you going through the hedge, and I figured you'd gone up or down the path. Down goes towards the road, up goes to the village. I thought that up was a better bet, and the colour of your skirt caught my eye as I passed this field.'

'Why did you want to see me? Anything special?'

He eyed her and her heart skipped a couple of beats. 'No special reason. I just wanted to see if you were OK.'

'That was kind of you. I'm fine, honestly.'

'It's not every day an orphan finds out she's not alone in the world.'

'No, but it's good news, and I'm going to visit my unknown second cousin as soon as I can. Did Eddie tell you she wanted to give me some pictures my dad painted and gave to her as a present when she got married?'

'Yes. I didn't realize your father was an artist.'

'A little-known one, but I'm looking forward to owning something that was his, even if it's only pictures.'

'I can understand that. You're still coming sailing with us on the weekend, I hope?'

Sara nodded. André was part of the outing, so they wouldn't be alone. 'Yes, I'm looking forward to it.'

He put one hand on the side to hoist himself up. 'Good! Well, I must get back to work.' He leaned forward and kissed her forehead before he leapt to his feet. 'See you later! Eddie and my mother are hoping for a quiet afternoon on the terrace once the removal men have left. Why don't you join them? I think my mother has a bottle of champagne in the fridge and fresh strawberries and cream.'

Heartened that he'd worried about how she was feeling, Sara managed a smile. 'Sounds good. I'll join them in a while.'

'Do that!' He stood tall and assertive in front of her with his thumbs stuck in the pockets of his jeans. With a final look at her face, he turned away and crossed the field with long, determined strides.

She watched as he marched along the edge of the field until he disappeared into the next one and went between the swaying straw-coloured grassland that plastered the incline of the field beyond. He didn't look back. Poppies and cornflowers brightened the undergrowth here and there. Sara loved him for what he was: a caring person who worked hard, enjoyed his life, and coped with difficulties as they came along. She wished she could be with him now and forevermore, even if she knew it was a silly, impossible dream. And the more time she spent with him, the greater the likelihood that she would betray her feelings.

Eddie's presence helped Sara during the next couple of days. There was someone else at the table to engage Nick in conversations, and to comment on local gossip or talk about estate business. Eddie was also ready if she wanted to go for a walk. There was no special reason for Nick to offer his company when the older man jumped to his feet like a shot.

Jannet and Eddie got on like a house on fire. It was easy to tell they shared the same attitude to life. Jannet was already looking forward to getting her plaster cast removed in a week or two.

As Saturday approached, Sara felt more nervous, but she vowed to hide her feelings from Nick as best she could. Eddie announced that he and Jannet had decided to meet up with them late in the afternoon after they returned from sailing, and they'd all have a meal in a local restaurant.

Sara set off with Nick straight after breakfast. They weren't alone for very long because Nick had arranged to pick up André on the way. 'Where are we going?' she asked.

Nick looked across at her briefly and smiled. 'A place called Perros-Guirec, on the Pink Granite Coast. André and the other part-owner, a friend of ours, berthed our boat there earlier in the week.'

'The other friend? Was he there the other evening?'

André chuckled. 'No, Gerald works in Paris now. He can't join us very often, but he was here last weekend. I left my car at our home marina, he drove his car to our setting-off point, and he cadged a ride back there with his brother to pick it up later.'

'What do you do for a living?' Sara asked André.

'Me? I run a supermarket with my father.'

'And you can take Saturday off? It must be the busiest day in the week.

Can you just have time off whenever you like?'

He laughed. 'More or less. It's a family concern. My parents still run it, and I have an elder sister who works there too. We also have a couple of employees, otherwise we wouldn't manage to keep the shelves filled and everything spick and span. I handle the ordering and payments. In other words, I do the office work, although I do help out in the shop in an emergency. We all cover for each other when one of us wants time off.'

'Lucky you!'

He nodded. 'It's only possible because it's a family concern. Nick tells me you're a librarian. Do you like your job?' He grinned at her and his eyes twinkled.

'On the whole, I do. People who borrow books are generally very nice. Is it far to wherever we're going?'

'It's not too far now,' Nick said. 'I hope you can swim? We have life-belts on board, but people who sail in small boats should be able to swim.'

'Yes, I can. I just hope I won't disgrace myself and be sick. I've never been on a sailing boat.'

Nick's brows lifted and the corners of his mouth turned up. 'That's one good thing about small boats — you can lean over the edge quite easily.'

André looked more worried, but then he shrugged his shoulders and gestured and commented in flowery language about a reckless driver who passed them only to have to brake hard when he reached the next set of traffic lights.

When they reached their destination, they boarded the small sailing boat called *Aphrodite*, which was smaller than Sara had imagined but big enough. The two men were a skilled team, and they were soon on their way out of the harbour. They seated Sara where she was not in their way, and she began to enjoy the feeling of gliding over the waves towards their destination. They explained they were heading towards a group of seven islands that looked like rounded dark shapes out at sea. The wind played havoc with Nick's hair, and Sara could tell he loved what he was doing.

He shouted above the sound of the wind. 'People often describe the islands as looking like whales from the land because of their humped shapes. They're home to a large number of seabirds, and there's also a small colony of grey seals.'

Once they were at sea and the boat's sails were set, he rummaged in a locker and handed Sara a pair of binoculars. She found that she loved the feeling of floating, sailing, and soaring across the waves. With her lungs full of fresh sea air, she felt no queasiness and was glad, for her own sake as well as Nick's and André's.

She could see they were busy sailing with the wind and heading towards the dark shapes. André was in charge of the tough little boat's large steering wheel. She'd noticed the small cabin at the front when they came on board, and they'd hastened to point out it was the 'bow' and not the 'front'. Nick was in charge of the boom, and he warned her to stay securely seated on the wooden side bench, and watch out that she ducked whenever necessary, otherwise she'd get bumped on the head or worse when he adjusted the boom to keep them on course.

They passed other boats now and then. The islands seemed to be popular tourist attractions. Looking back, the very rugged and magnificent coastline already seemed far off. Sara concentrated her attention on the islands in front of them. Sailing past one after the other, she saw cormorants on rocky outcrops, and huge numbers of gannets on one island. There were so many of them that the island itself seemed white from a distance. Nick told her that gannets were incredibly faithful to the mate they'd chosen. André commented they must be very stupid birds. Nick handed her a mug of coffee from a flask he'd brought along and went to give

André a mug as he sat at the wheel, then returned to her side.

They sat hip to hip and inches apart. Sara gripped the mug tightly. 'Do you change tasks sometimes?'

'You mean me steering, him at the boom? Yes, of course we do. We have no set jobs. It depends on how we feel.' He pointed to the island they were passing. 'Look at the tourists over there. They're having a picnic. The seagulls are so used to them that they just swoop down and eat from people's hands.'

'You've been here before?'

'Um, a few times. We like the sailing conditions around this part of the coastline. It's a challenge because conditions can be rough sometimes, although they're good today.'

Sara pushed the hair out of her face and smiled at him. 'I was just thinking that you're an estate manager who spends his time growing things on a farm. You live inland away from the coast, and you still love sailing.'

'Yes, I love the sea. Are you enjoying yourself?'

She nodded enthusiastically. 'It's great. No sea-sickness, I have nothing to do, and we have good weather. It couldn't be better.'

They didn't go on land anywhere, but sailed out beyond the island where the winds were stronger. A couple of hours later they made the return journey. They re-entered port with sea-salt on their skin, and Sara had a headful of special memories. She wished she'd remembered to take her camera along.

By the time they'd secured the boat and left the jetty, the afternoon was well advanced. They went searching for the Hotel Manoir du Sphinx, in which was the restaurant that Eddie had picked out on the internet. Eddie and Jannet were already there, enjoying a glass of red wine on the terrace. Jannet waved as they arrived.

The meal was wonderful, and they were all hungry. Each of them chose a different fish dish, and Jannet tried bits of everyone's to figure out the recipes so that she could try them at home one day. They lingered over coffee and a last glass of wine before they set off for home again.

Sara could have gone with Jannet and Eddie, but she'd come with Nick and André and she wanted the memory of the day with Nick to end with him too. There was more traffic on the road on the return journey, but that was to be expected. Tourists were busy discovering the charms of Brittany, and local people were on their Saturday outings.

They dropped André outside his flat and continued on. Near the château, the traffic thinned out. Nick parked the jeep neatly on the side of one of the outbuildings, where he always left it. He leaned back in his seat and folded his hands behind his head for a moment.

Sara didn't want the day to end. She turned slightly and said, 'Thank you for a lovely time, Nick. I'll always remember it.'

'My pleasure! We must do it again soon.'

She didn't think that was likely to happen. Before long, she'd be far away again. She stared ahead through the windscreen and didn't notice that Nick had come round to her side and was holding out his hand. She took it and he helped her out. He stood in the fading daylight for a moment, looking down at her, then did what she longed for him to do.

The kiss was gentle and all she wanted. She didn't resist; the temptation was too great. She should have said something, but she just turned away and went towards the house. Nick followed. Inside, she heard Eddie in the sitting room.

'I need a shower,' she said, and ran upstairs.

Nick wondered if he was misjudging the situation. Why did he feel she was deliberately slipping away from him when he needed to find out was if there was any hope for them?

16

Sunday was always lazy. Breakfast lasted as long as it was wanted. Jannet usually had a day off from cooking and they ate something she'd frozen. Everyone idled the hours away doing what they wanted to. Sara skipped breakfast and just enjoyed a cup of coffee. The sun was coming up as she viewed the surrounding countryside from the terrace. The silence and beauty were balm for the soul. Jannet came out with her own coffee and mentioned that Nick was tinkering on some old car he was restoring in the barn.

Sara was tempted to join him, but decided it was more sensible to go for a walk. She set off through the meadow behind the house and soon found herself on the edge of, and then inside, a patch of dense forest. Sunshine fought its way through the branches, and a green coverlet of leaves spread far above her. The ground was a soft carpet of mosses and cast-off fir needles. Sara tried to pay attention where she was going, although it was more difficult than she expected. In the end she thought she would have to use the sun as her guide, although she also realized it would change position during the course of the day.

Reaching the other side of the small forest, she found herself looking across a number of fields that spread out before her on all sides. The warm wind rustled her skirt and pressed her T-shirt to her body. It would have been a perfect moment if she hadn't seen Madeleine crossing one of the fields and heading in her direction. When Madeleine saw her, she hesitated for a moment, but then quickened her pace. Sara remained standing. She didn't particularly want to talk to the woman, and hoped Madeleine would head off in another direction before they met, but instead she deliberately quickened her pace towards her.

Sara gave her a stiff-lipped smile. 'Morning, Madeleine!'

'Morning!' There was a distinct hardening of Madeleine's eyes as she replied.

Sara clenched her mouth tighter. Madeleine didn't like her, and Sara knew why: it was about Nick. She was anxious to escape, but politeness cemented her to the spot. She searched for something sensible to say. 'They're all relaxing at the château. I decided to go for a walk. I've never been in this direction before.'

'I expect you thought it would be nice to check things?' Madeleine's chin jutted forward aggressively.

Sara stiffened and was momentarily abashed. 'What do you mean?'

The other woman laughed falsely. 'Oh, come off it. Don't pretend you don't understand.'

Sara's unease increased. 'I'm not pretending. I don't know what you're talking about or why you're being so unfriendly. What's wrong?'

Madeleine shook her head, tossing her hair in a gesture of defiance. 'You know very well what's wrong. How do you say it in English? Dominique *être un bon parti*, and you're after him!'

Silence reigned for a second or two and Sara ran her tongue over her lips. 'You're mistaken. I am not chasing Nick, Madeleine.'

'Huh! Why would someone like you return to the château to stay for weeks unless they had a special reason?'

Sara managed to shrug and tried to speak calmly. 'I came back because Jannet asked me to. It had nothing to do with Nick.' She twisted her hands together and stood her ground.

Madeleine looked down quickly. When she looked at Sara again, her eyes were sharp and accusing. 'Before you turned up with your innocent eyes and English accent, things were fine between me and Nick. Now he doesn't have time for me anymore.'

'You can't blame me for that,

Madeleine. It's not my fault. Perhaps you should ask Nick what's wrong.'

Madeleine's voice lashed out at her. 'We had a silent agreement before you came on the scene. He was mine!'

Sara blushed. 'Was he? Then you have no reason to worry, have you?'

'I felt sure he was about to suggest we get married. Now he's been distracted, hoping for a quick affair with you, but it won't lead anywhere. He loves me.'

With a lump in her throat the size of a lemon, Sara felt weak and vulnerable. 'Don't be silly, Madeleine. We're not having an affair. I'm a visitor, and he's been a kind host on a couple of occasions.' Ignoring her memories of his kisses, she added, 'There's nothing romantic about it. Maybe you should just trust Nick.'

She shrugged. 'Men are men! Dominique is as pliable as all the rest. If something is presented to him on a plate, he'll eat it!'

Madeleine's tone infuriated Sara.

'He's not shallow and heartless. I don't believe Nick would behave like that.' She paused. 'But you know him best. If what you say was true, I'm surprised you don't seem to mind the idea of him cheating on you.'

'I'm just rational and sensible. No one expects their husband to be faithful these days. Temptation is everywhere, but as a matter of fact I do happen to like Dominique, and we were meant for each other since we were small. Everyone around here knows that. I just wanted to remind you and tell you so. If he shows interest, it doesn't mean a thing. It's merely a flirt, an affair, a quick liaison. Then the minute you return to England, he'll come back to me again, assuring me I'm the only one. Don't build up any hopes!' Madeleine didn't conceal the insolent tone in her voice.

Sara was numb at first, then felt increasing anger mixed with shock. She coloured fiercely and glowered at Madeleine. 'You're not talking about love; you're talking about habits and bowing to convention. If that's true, I feel sorry for you both. A life founded on empty emotions is doomed. You'll both be miserable. If you love him, you'd want him to be happy, and you wouldn't want to marry him unless he loved you. It sounds as if you just want him because he happens to be your neighbour and because he's suitable. Centuries ago, they called such arrangements 'marriages of convenience', and they rarely produced marital bliss. If you love Nick, that's fine, but don't pretend he's a womanizer or that you can control him. He isn't, and you can't. And don't blame me if your relationship isn't working out.' She turned away abruptly and went back into the wood, not watching where she was going and stumbling now and then. She kept going for a while, until she felt she was far enough away from Madeleine's spiteful words; then she sat down on a log and buried her face in her hands.

Madeleine was jealous. Sara could understand that, because any woman was jealous and angry when they believed someone was stealing their man. But Sara hadn't stolen him. Why did Madeleine believe she had endangered their unspoken agreement? Nick had been kind to a stranger. Madeleine didn't like it, and she'd construed the situation incorrectly.

Sara had already decided when she came to help Jannet that more than friendship with Nick was not a good idea, and a risky undertaking. It could only be a holiday romance. An affair might be simple to begin with, when it was short-term and devoid of emotion. She'd done her best to avoid getting too involved with Nick, because she knew it would lead nowhere. If she'd thrown all caution to the wind and let things happen, it wouldn't have been what she'd wanted. That wasn't the kind of person she was. She wanted all or nothing.

Pain squeezed her heart as she

thought of him, and she tried to control her disappointment. She reflected that fate had once again dealt her an unexpected blow. She'd found a man she loved but could never have. Suddenly she noticed that tears were running down her cheeks, and she brushed them away quickly. She had to get away from the château. It wouldn't be right to face Nick, Jannet, and the community day after day, knowing they thought she was holding out for an affair. Madeleine's words had demonstrated just how silly it was to stay. Jannet could manage on her own now, and she'd soon be out of her plaster cast. Eddie would be here to support her for a while longer. Her leaving had to appear natural.

There was no more sunshine fighting through the greenery as she began to look for the way back to the château. She caught glimpses of clouds through the leaves high above her now, and they suited her present mood much better. As she went, she thought about an excuse. How she could leave without causing any suspicion? She had to detour now and then until she found the way, but she didn't worry about getting lost. She soon found herself near her starting point behind the château.

When she reached them, Jannet and Eddie were still where she'd left them, sitting on the terrace. She managed a smile and said jokingly. 'You look like an old married couple.'

Jannet coloured, and Sara suddenly realized something could be developing between them. Well, why not? They were both free, and they were both lovely people who got on extremely well.

Eddie tried to distract them all. He pointed into the far distance. 'Look at that. It looks like a bird of prey to me.'

Jannet hastened to answer. 'Yes, could be. We often see them circling the fields.' She looked at Sara. 'Madeleine was just here. She came to collect Nick. Apparently one of their friends is in hospital, and Madeleine thought Nick should visit him. She wouldn't let him off the hook, so Nick gave in, washed his hands and went. He should have at least changed his jeans, but Madeleine was very anxious to get away.' Looking at Sara's expression, she asked, 'Is something wrong, Sara? You look very pale.'

'Do I? No, there's nothing wrong.'

Jannet reflected for a moment, then nodded. 'Eddie and I were just thinking about going to a musical festival this afternoon. It's taking place over the weekend, with traditional Breton music and dance.'

Sara was glad to hear of a possible escape route for a few hours. 'I'd love to come, if I'm not in the way.'

'Of course not! I was just about to freshen up, and then we can go.'

Late afternoon, when they returned after an enjoyable insight into traditional dancing, with music that included the Breton bagpipes, there was still no sign of Nick. Sara was glad. It gave her even more time to adjust before she had to face him again.

They had a cold supper on the terrace: a pâté, green salad, crusty fresh bread and lots of local cheeses. They lingered, chatting about what they'd seen. Sara helped to clear the table. Jannet said Nick could make his own food if he needed something when he came in.

Sara excused herself as the sun began to set behind the fields. 'I'm going to have a shower and an extended read before I put out the light. Goodnight.'

She had just reached her room when she heard the front door closing. She leaned against her door and slid to the ground, feeling defeated and miserable.

17

Sara postponed going downstairs the next morning until she was sure Nick had left. She hadn't slept well, and was still trying to think of a plausible excuse as to why she must leave. Down in the kitchen, Jannet was checking the post that had just arrived via the post van. Eddie was out somewhere.

'Oh, that's good!' Jannet said as she read a letter she was holding. 'The solicitors say they've completed the negotiations for Maldon House. The wellness company wants the house, and Watson's Building Company has bought the plot of land on the other side of the stream. That means the village won't change much. The new houses can't be seen from the road or the house, there are lots of trees and greenery in between. Apparently they can get access to the new site via the road on the other side too, so everyone should be happy with the results.' She folded the letter and put it on the table. 'My doctor confirms that I can get the plaster cast removed next week too, so I almost feel like opening a bottle of champagne. I must find Eddie and tell him the good news.'

Sara smiled. 'That's great; he'll be happy. He can dissolve the protest group. Where is he?'

'Out in the barn. He wanted to unpack some of the furniture to make sure it hasn't been damaged.'

'You wait here. Propelling your wheelchair through the gravel is hard going. I'll get him and you can tell him the news. We'll be back for a celebratory coffee in five minutes.'

Jannet nodded and began to roll towards the coffee machine.

As Sara had expected, Eddie was relieved. 'I'm so glad,' he said. 'I was afraid we'd end up with us opposing Jannet. This solution will suit everyone.'

That evening, dinner was a very

cheerful occasion, and Sara could join in without too many qualms. Eddie told Nick about their visit to the music festival the day before and then that the problems with Maldon House had been solved. The meal flowed along with no hitches. Whenever Nick's eyes met hers, Sara's heart somersaulted, and she did her best to keep her expression neutral. She thought she saw puzzlement on his face sometimes. She tried to concentrate on Eddie's conversation and Jannet's bantering.

After they were finished and the dishes washed and stored away, they settled down to an evening in the sitting room. Eddie and Nick wanted to watch the evening news. Jannet picked up some mending work, and Sara pretended to be busy with her book. If anyone had noticed, they'd have seen her book was upside down. She eventually noticed herself and casually turned it round. As she did so, the letter from her second cousin in Wales fell out. She picked it up and read it through again. Her relative had included her telephone number. Suddenly Sara realized that was her way out. She could get in touch and explain she only had a couple of days' holiday left, and would like to meet her straight away. It was plausible. She felt decidedly happier.

Nick turned from the television and towards her. 'André and I are going to pick up the *Aphrodite* and sail her back to the local marina. I'm picking him up on Friday lunchtime and plan to be back home sometime on Saturday. We can sleep on board. The cabin's a bit cramped, but if the weather's good, it's even possible to sleep on deck. Want to come?'

Sara was lost for words for a moment. 'Thanks, that's very kind, but you'll enjoy your sailing better without me getting in the way. You probably need plenty of room to manoeuvre if you're sailing a long distance. Have a great trip, and be careful!'

He considered her thoughtfully for a

moment before he shrugged his broad shoulders. 'OK! Another time, perhaps?'

She gave him a hesitant smile. 'Perhaps.'

★ ★ ★

On Wednesday, Sara told Eddie and Jannet she was leaving. Jannet protested, 'I hoped you'd stay at least until my plaster cast comes off at the end of next week. Won't you put off the visit to your relatives for just another week or two, just to please me?'

Sara shook her head. 'Eddie will take you there and bring you back. You don't need me anymore. You'll stay, won't you, Eddie?'

Eddie looked a little perplexed, but he nodded. 'Of course! If it helps.'

Jannet frowned and continued, 'I'm disappointed, Sara. We're good friends, and you've helped me all this time; and now you're going to leave before I'm back on my feet again.'

Eddie reached out and touched her arm. 'Steady on! You know how much finding her relatives means to Sara. It's understandable that she wants to contact them as soon as possible, isn't it? If this relation has invited her, I can understand why she needs to go. Sara hasn't been bedded in roses all her life. She deserves to feel she's not alone in this world. Hilda is next to useless.'

Sara laughed softly. 'That's not true, Eddie. Hilda did her best, and she does care for me.'

Jannet's expression changed and she looked contrite. 'Yes, you're right, Eddie. I'm just being selfish. I'm so fond of Sara, and I forgot she has a life of her own elsewhere.'

Sara got up and bent down to hug her. 'I love you too, and I'll never forget your kindness and hospitality. We'll keep in touch, I promise. You'll probably have to come over soon to sign some legal papers. Eddie can be host again, and we'll go to see more famous gardens.'

Jannet's eyes were misty. She nodded.

That evening, when Nick was about to begin his meal, Jannet told him Sara had decided to leave on Friday. His surprise and ensuing vexation were evident as he viewed Sara across the table. There was a distinct hardening of his eyes when he said, 'A bit sudden, isn't it?' The words were full of sarcasm.

To her annoyance, Sara started to blush and stuttered. 'Surely it's not that surprising, is it, Nick? Your mother invited me for a couple of weeks, and I've been here a long time already. Eddie can replace me until your mother's back on her own two feet again. I hope that I've helped, although Jannet is so independent despite her broken leg that I often feel like there's not much for me to do.' She smiled at Jannet and then returned her glance to him. 'I want to visit my lost relations in Wales before my holiday finishes. I won't be able to get away until the autumn if I don't go now.'

He drawled with distinct mockery,

'Of course. Wales is incredibly far away from your home, isn't it? And your employers also have you working seven days a week — never a weekend free?'

His mother interjected, 'Nick, don't be rude. Sara is entitled to do what she likes. I've enjoyed having her here, and she's been a great help. I hope to see her again soon.'

Nick and Sara stared at each other across the ensuing silence. Nick's skin was taut across his nose and around his mouth. If Sara was hoping for softer words, she was disappointed.

He threw his napkin on the table and got up. 'I've just remembered — I've promised to meet someone. I'm not hungry anyway. Don't wait any longer with the rest of the meal.' He got up and turned away without waiting for a reply, then went out and closed the door behind him firmly.

Eddie tried to ease the tension. 'You know the route to the ferry, Sara, so it'll be no problem for you to get there on time. When does it leave on Friday?'

She bit her lip and concentrated. 'Two o'clock. That gives me plenty of time to get there, and to be off the ferry and home before it's too late.'

She managed to finish her meal while listening to the other two chatting about inconsequential subjects that filled the silence. Each forkful felt like a rock as it went down. She was grateful that they were trying to ignore Nick's comments. Eddie and Jannet said they'd manage the washing up, so Sara decided to escape to her room.

She met Nick coming down the stairs. He stiffened when he saw her, and gave her a look as sharp as a knife. She tried to retain her composure and managed a smile that wasn't returned.

As they passed, he said, 'Unfortunately I find that Madeleine wasn't mistaken when she said you were someone who played with men's emotions and took advantage of people.'

Sara turned and, feeling infuriated, replied. 'And of course Madeleine is an expert on emotions and people, isn't she?'

His temper flared. 'She's known me a hell of a lot longer than you have. I trust her judgement.'

Sara felt extraordinarily empty. She didn't want to fight him. If he believed Madeleine was so intrinsically good, they probably would end up married one day. She couldn't help adding, 'I don't play with anyone's emotions Nick. I never have. I don't know what's bothering you so much, and I don't understand why you're angry with me either. I don't belong here — you know it, and so do I.'

He shrugged, his mouth set in a hard line. 'So it seems.' The unwelcome tension stretched even tighter between them as he eyed her and then bounded down the remaining stairs. When he reached the door, he threw it open, didn't look back, and slammed it behind him.

Sara raced to her room and leaned against the door. Her heart was pounding and she had to swallow a lump in her throat. Nothing she did could stop the tears flowing. Minutes later, she tried to remove the red from her eyes by cooling them with water. She couldn't hide in her room all night. When she began to think logically again, she wondered if it wasn't better this way. Nick was angry with her; angry about the way she was deserting his mother, and probably that he'd kissed her. That meant he also thought she was a flirt. It wouldn't matter what he thought about her once she left anyway, and it would be easier for her if she remembered his angry face instead of his smiles. She grabbed her book, brushed her hair back into shape, and straightened her shoulders.

18

The next morning when they were alone, Jannet asked Sara if something unusual had happened to annoy Nick.

'No, nothing special that I know about.'

She tilted her head to the side. 'He's like a bear with a sore head this morning. Does it have something to do with last Sunday, when you came back from your walk looking upset? Did you meet Madeleine? Did she say something hurtful? She turned up here just before you came, and I thought it was funny you two hadn't met when you were out.'

Sara's heart sank. She didn't want to start any trouble, especially now she was leaving. 'Don't worry, Jannet. There's nothing for you to fret about.'

She felt sad on Friday when she said her goodbyes. Jannet asked earnestly,

'You will come back one day, won't you?'

Sara smiled, knowing she wouldn't. 'I'll try! Good luck with the plaster cast. I hope your leg has healed properly. I'll see you when you get home, Eddie.'

He nodded. Sara hugged Jannet and got into her car. She hadn't seen much of Nick since Wednesday evening. When she did, he had been coldly distant. He was clearly avoiding her as much as he could. He hadn't been home Thursday evening, and she wouldn't see him today either because she was leaving for home and he was going on the sailing trip with André. He hadn't left any goodbyes with Jannet, either. Perhaps it was better that way, but it hurt.

★   ★   ★

Back home again, Sara told Aunt Hilda about the letter from her Welsh relations. Hilda spluttered and tried to explain why she'd ignored earlier letters, never mentioning them to Sara.

241

'I was afraid I'd lose you, Sara. I'm sorry! I realize now it was wrong of me.'

Sara knew she'd forgive her. Aunt Hilda would never change, and she probably had wanted the best for Sara. Sometimes she aimed wide of the mark, but there was no point in them quarrelling. It was punishment enough for Aunt Hilda to know Sara had other relations who also cared.

Sara called to see Kelly that evening. She was about to leave to meet Mark again, so there wasn't much time to talk. Sara could tell her friend was happier than she'd ever seen her before, and it seemed that Mark was attracted to her as well, so this time Kelly was serious.

The next morning, Sara left for the address in Wales. As she drove through the countryside and reached the Gower, she was glad to think of things other than Dominique Rogard. Her cousin Morgan lived in a beautiful village near the coast. If she could only forget Nick! But she couldn't, and knew she never would. She couldn't sleep properly. She kept dreaming that he was walking away, and no matter how hard she tried to catch him, he faded further and further from her. How long would it take before she felt like her old self again? she wondered.

Sara liked her Welsh cousin, and she was pleased when Morgan insisted that she stay until Monday. They went for long walks together, and Sara learned about her father's family. Morgan gave Sara copies of family photos and made her promise to come to the next family get-together. Her father's framed paintings were beautiful reminders of someone she couldn't recall, and she already treasured them.

Sara set out for a walk on her own on Sunday afternoon, as Morgan wanted to visit an ailing elderly neighbour. The wind was whistling on the headland, but the air was sweet with the smell of grass as she walked at a leisurely pace along the well-trodden path. She buried her hands in her anorak pocket and looked out over the buoyant waters down below. It was a splendid view. She was actually looking forward to work in a week's time; it would help her think of other things.

Apart from some people out walking their dogs, there was no one else in sight. She stopped and sat down on a protruding grey rock. Down below, the sea swirled around a myriad of other rocks. Once again, her thoughts wandered back to Nick as she watched the waves without seeing them.

'Sara!'

The voice was familiar, but she thought she was dreaming until she turned, and her breath caught in her throat when she saw Nick. The colour left her face. 'What are you doing here?'

'I had to come. I had see you. I hope you'll forgive me for the stupid way I acted before you left. I was angry, but for the wrong reasons.'

Feeling flustered, she said softly, 'You didn't need to follow me to tell me that. How did you find me?'

'Your aunt told me where you were in Wales, and your cousin just told me you were out here, walking on the headland.'

Sara rose and stood motionless as she studied the face she loved. He was neatly dressed in a casual brown leather jacket with a checked shirt that peeped out of its collar, and beige gabardine trousers. 'Why are you here?'

'To say I'm sorry! To explain why I was so angry. Even before you said you were leaving I was unhappy, because I thought I'd completely misjudged the situation. I thought things were going to be perfect between us, but I never got the chance to find out where we stood, and then all of a sudden you wanted to run. My pride told me there was no point in trying to change your mind or ask how you felt. Then Madeleine tried to make things worse by criticising you in all sorts of ways. But that didn't stop me thinking about you. Even though I didn't know how to cope, I was angry at her and told her never to condemn you in my presence again.

'While we were out sailing, I talked to André about how I felt about you; about how you left me breathless and speechless, and that I'd never met anyone I wanted so much. He told me that if I didn't come after you and talk things through, I'd regret it for the rest of my life. Well, he was right. I love you, Sara, and nothing anyone says or does can alter that. I never thought love would take over my whole being, but it has. If I can't have you, life won't have much purpose anymore.'

The ground under Sara's feet seemed to lurch. 'You love me?'

He nodded. 'More than I can say. I can't remember when I realized — I just know that tomorrow, next week, next year, and the rest of my life will be pointless unless you love me and want to share my life with me.'

Sara's hand went to her throat and he placed his own over it. 'But — but — ' she stammered.

He moved his finger to her lips. 'No

buts. Just forgive me. Do I have a chance? Or was I just imagining that the way I feel about you is how you feel about me too?'

She leaned towards him, her delight growing. She smoothed his hair with her hand and watched him carefully. 'Of course I forgive you, but I'm not sure what for. Nick, I'm just as mixed up. I couldn't imagine that under the circumstances we'd have more than a holiday romance, and I loved you too much to want a meaningless affair. I had to leave because I couldn't see how we could achieve the kind of future I wanted.'

The moment she admitted she loved him, his eyes sparkled and he laughed loudly. 'I see one kind of future for us. I see two people enjoying a loving, lasting marriage and life together. I didn't think it would ever happen to me, but I know I'm just an empty shell without you, Sara.' His kiss sent spirals of ecstasy through her. Then he recaptured her lips, and his kiss was more demanding this time. Her eager response left him in no doubt.

Sara placed her palms against his chest and looked up at him. She was almost pleading. 'But Nick, how can it work? I love you more than my life, but you're a farmer with responsibilities, and when it comes to farming I hardly know anything. What's more, you're French; I'm British. And you have a long-standing circle of friends who may not want to accept me.'

He silenced her with his finger again and grinned. 'You don't have to know anything about farming. Do you think I expect you to drive a tractor or shoulder a hoe in a field of cauliflowers or carrots? And your French is perfect; that's no problem. Furthermore, my friends will like you — and if any of them don't, they're not my friends. André thinks you're the bee's knees already.'

'And Madeleine?'

He lifted her hand and kissed the tips of her fingers. It sent gentle currents of desire through her. 'What about Madeleine? I thought she was one of my friends, but I'll never forget the way she tried to run you down, and how I fell for it. She tried to drive us apart, but love was stronger in the end. I never thought of her in a romantic way, and I never promised her anything either. If she reckoned on something else, that's her problem, not mine.'

'She's a neighbour.'

He shrugged. 'She either accepts you and makes you welcome, or stays away. I realize there'll always be tension between us now if she stays, but I think when she sees how happy we are, she'll move away. That would suit us better.'

Sara couldn't deny her desire to be with him. There was a tingling in the pit of her stomach. Still, this seemed a good time to put many questions out in the open. 'But your estate and her parents' farm ... they border each other.'

'And?' He pushed her hair behind

her ears, and the smouldering flame she saw in his eyes made her spirit soar.

'I heard people suggest how their farm would be added to yours if you married Madeleine.'

'Rumours, rumours, rumours! Reality is something else. I don't need more land — I have more than I need. But I do need a certain English woman who is beautiful, kind, caring, reliable . . . and who I just heard loves me in return.'

'What about your mother?'

Tongue in cheek, he said, 'I suppose you're already worrying about all the mother-in-law clichés you've heard? Well I love you, I love her in another way, and she loves you already. Not as much as I do, but enough. I think she hoped that we'd pair up when she asked you to come back to help her. She's crafty.'

'You think so?'

He nodded. 'She knew you were right for me. We'll have to split the château with her in some way so that we lead separate lives. She's not quarrelsome, but she's lived there since she got married, and it would be better if you and I could have some privacy. I think she'll be absolutely delighted if I tell her we're going to get married.' He paused. 'From the way things are going, I can imagine that perhaps she and Eddie will make a go of it one day too.'

Sara's eyes widened. He was already talking about marriage. 'Really? Do you mind?'

'Why should I? I'm happy if I have you. I want her to be happy, and I like Eddie. They'll probably end up commuting back and forth between France and England.'

'Eddie has two children, but I'm sure they'd want him to be happy too.'

'Good, a couple more additions to the family. But the most important addition is you. Sara, will you give up your life with your aunt and come to France to make me happy? You have another week's holiday. Spend it with me. I'll take time off too, and we can be together all day. We'll work out the rest later, but I don't intend to wait forever to have you by my side day and night. Until then, it's ferry crossings every weekend. I'm almost resigned to being with Aunt Hilda.'

Joy bubbled in Sara's responsive laugh, and it shone in her eyes. 'I already want you, Nick. I don't care what Aunt Hilda or anyone else thinks. The kind of life I've always dreamed about is just beginning for me, and you are all I want.'

Sara felt how love was encircling her like the scent of perfume from a bottle — only this was a perfume that would never fade away. Dominique Rogard was her dream come true.

We do hope that you have enjoyed reading this large print book.

Did you know that all of our titles are available for purchase?

We publish a wide range of high quality large print books including:
Romances, Mysteries, Classics
General Fiction
Non Fiction and Westerns

Special interest titles available in large print are:
The Little Oxford Dictionary
Music Book, Song Book
Hymn Book, Service Book

Also available from us courtesy of Oxford University Press:
Young Readers' Dictionary
(large print edition)
Young Readers' Thesaurus
(large print edition)

For further information or a free brochure, please contact us at:
Ulverscroft Large Print Books Ltd.,
The Green, Bradgate Road, Anstey,
Leicester, LE7 7FU, England.
Tel: (00 44) **0116 236 4325**
Fax: (00 44) **0116 234 0205**

SECRETS OF MELLIN COVE

Rena George

After Wenna discovers a shocking family secret, she flies to the comfort of her beloved Cornish moors. What can she do? If she reveals the terrible truth, her family will be ruined. If she does nothing, she could be condemning the crew of a sailing ship to death. Perhaps she should confide in the tall stranger who rides past her every day, always casting an interested glance in her direction. But would he understand, or would he go straight to the authorities? No, she couldn't trust a stranger . . . or could she?

RUNAWAY LOVE

Fay Wentworth

When Emma flees to Leigh Manor to escape the pain of a broken romance, she finds that life there as a secretary to Alex Baron is not as simple as she anticipated. An unfortunate encounter between herself, Alex and a bull heralds the start of a fiery relationship. And what is the mystery behind the charming façade of Blake, Alex's assistant? As Emma's new job gets off to a rocky start, she soon finds herself wondering who she can trust — and whether coming to Leigh Manor was a good idea . . .

GIFT OF THE NILE

Heidi Sullivan

Amber Davis has always loved hearing about her father's archaeological excavations, and is thrilled when she is finally allowed to accompany the professor on an expedition. As she begins her Egyptian adventure, she meets expatriates Lachlan and his son James. Amber is drawn to the artistic and bohemian James, but is concerned about the lecherous eye of his father. When things begin to go very wrong during the trip, can Amber keep her head . . . and her heart?

TRUSTING A STRANGER

Sarah Purdue

Clara Radley's life is all about her studies until she is woken in the night by hammering on her front door. Into her world steps handsome US Special Agent Jack Henry, who tells her that her life is in danger and his job is to protect her. Henry has been sent by her biological father — a US Army General who Clara has never even met. How can she trust this stranger? But what choice does she have?

THE TREGELIAN HOARD

Ellie Holmes

With her engagement in tatters, Jonquil Jones, a Portable Antiquities specialist, moves to Cornwall for a fresh start. When a golden torc that has lain hidden underground for centuries is unearthed, she can feel her soul stirring with excitement. Is it a single find, or part of an extraordinary treasure trove? It's Jonquil's job to find out. But there is one problem: Sebastian Ableyard, who reported the find, is the man Jonquil holds responsible for the break-up of her engagement . . .